# The D[illegible]
# Crescent Dunes



## The Guardians of Elestra #3

Thom Jones

Peekaboo Pepper Books

ISBN: 0615503071
ISBN-13: 978-0615503073

# DEDICATION

This book is dedicated to Dinara, the early morning kicking bandit, Aidan, whose imaginary world is very much like Elestra, minus the mushrooms, Galen, electric guitarist extraordinaire, and Linda, who doesn't really resemble Tobungus (she's much taller).

The Desert of the Crescent Dunes, Guardians of Elestra #3

Also available in the Guardians of Elestra series:

#1 The Dark City
#2 The Giants of the Baroka Valley
#4 The Seven Pillars of Tarook
#5 The Eye of the Red Dragon
#6 The Misty Peaks of Dentarus (Summer 2011)

To learn more about Elestra, including maps, history, Tobungus' blog, Glabber's menu, and contests that allow readers to submit ideas for new characters, places, or other magical things, please visit:

**www.guardiansofelestra.com**

# CONTENTS

# 1 Here, Kitty, Kitty!

*"Derek. . . Derek,"* an old, soft voice whispered. Derek Hughes stirred from a restful sleep to see who was calling him. *"Derek."* The voice sounded so old that he imagined the words struggling through a layer of dust.

"Who's there?" Derek asked nervously.

*"Derek,"* the voice sounded tired. *"The library. . . the ancient archives. . . prophecy."*

Derek rubbed his sleepy eyes and mumbled, "the library?"

*"The ancient archives."* The voice trailed off as it whispered, *"Gula Badu."*

"What?" Derek shot back. There was no reply. "What's Gula Badu?"

Silence filled the room. Derek looked around in the darkness, trying to see any movement. After several minutes, he realized that there was no one else in the room other than his twin sister Deanna. He got out of bed and walked across to the big cushy chair by the window. He spent the last hour before the sun rose trying to figure out what the voice was telling him.

He thought back to the night when he and Deanna had seen their grandfather disappear into the old lantern in their backyard and learned about the magical adventures that awaited them in this strange land of Elestra. It was on that night that their grandfather told them that they were the last of the Mystical Guardians. They were Elestra's only hope to recover the lost moonstones, powerful magical jewels which would enable them to defeat the evil wizard Eldrack.

It still seemed like a dream. It had been exciting, but he missed his parents, even though the great wizard Iszarre explained that his father must stay out of Elestra to remain safe.

Iszarre had arranged for them to stay in a room upstairs at Glabber's Grub Hut. He had even placed a magical spell on the room to make it look exactly like the room the twins shared back home. Derek could hear Glabber clanging pots and dishes in the kitchen below and hoped that the sounds from the diner would wake Deanna.

But it wasn't until the morning had replaced the long, dark night that Deanna stirred in her soft bed, instinctively hiding from the sun's rays beneath the billowing white blankets that covered her like a sky full of clouds.

"Come on, Deanna," Derek called. "Get up. We've got a lot to do today."

"Hold on," Deanna replied groggily. "I'm trying to get used to the light."

"Deanna," Derek said, "It's cloudy today. Get out of bed so we can get to the library."

Derek and Deanna had to go to the library to learn about the Desert of the Crescent Dunes. Iszarre had hinted that this was the location of the next moonstone. For the first time, they would be leaving Magia, so they wanted to gather as much information as possible. Derek also wanted to find out if the voice that had awakened him was leading him to something important.

Deanna finally pushed back the covers and slowly climbed out of bed. As Derek waited impatiently for Deanna to gather her clothes, he looked out the window toward a park they had seen on their walks back to Glabber's Grub Hut from the Tower of the Moons.

Each of the park's entrances had a small fountain with a statue of one of Elestra's great wizards from the past. They had hoped to spend some time in the park to learn more about Elestra's history, but for now, they had to focus on gathering the moonstones before the dark wizard Eldrack got to them.

As Derek stood deep in thought, looking at the fountain, he saw something that he couldn't quite explain. "Huh?" he mumbled, as he started to piece together what was happening.

Deanna looked over and saw Derek's look of surprise. "What's wrong, Derek?" she asked.

"I'll be right back," Derek answered as he grabbed the Wand of Ondarell and ran out the door. He flew down the stairs and out into the street toward the fountain. There, he saw his friend Tobungus, the mushroom man, setting a plate next to the fountain's outer stone wall. A foot-long fish rested on the plate. Tobungus could barely hold back his laughter as he put his devious plan into motion.

Off to the right, Zorell, the talking cat, was crouching and ready to pounce on the fishy feast. He was so desperate to get to the fish that he didn't stop to think how odd Tobungus' actions were. To the left, hidden by bushes, two large, extremely hungry looking saber-tooth dogs crouched, drooling and ready to pounce once Zorell made his move.

"Out of the way, Tobungus," Derek shouted as he raised the wand.

Tobungus was already on his way to a hiding place where he could watch Zorell walk into his trap. He didn't seem to hear Derek's command. But, he definitely noticed what happened next.

*"Gigantum pisce,"* Derek yelled as the fanged beasts leapt from behind the bushes. A flash of blue light hit the fish and it began to swell. Its tail inflated first, followed by the rest of its body. Soon, the gray fish was nearly fifteen feet long and looked like a small blimp.

Derek rarely used the wand, partly because Deanna was so skilled with it, and partly because he was not very confident in his magical abilities. He smiled to himself, thinking that he had finally made a spell work exactly as he wanted it to.

The hungry saber-toothed dogs tripped over one another as they backed away from the giant mutant fish. They turned quickly and fled, knocking several people to the ground along the cobblestone street. Zorell ran to Derek's side which made Derek feel more confident in his use of the wand.

"No! Wait! Come back," Tobungus shouted. He quickly fell silent, however, when he turned to see Derek staring and Zorell glaring at him. "What?" He asked a little too innocently. Zorell hissed and prepared to pounce.

"Alright, you two," Derek said, moving to stand between Tobungus and Zorell. "Let's go get some breakfast and talk this over."

"Aren't you going to do something with the fish?" Zorell asked.

Derek turned around and saw a growing number of people in the park stopping and staring in amazement at the massive fish. "Actually, I don't know the counterspell," he whispered, as they hurried back to Glabber's Grub Hut.

Along the way, Derek had to walk between his two friends. Zorell had his claws out. Tobungus had a squirt bottle filled with a brown liquid that smelled like burned pickles and wet dog aimed at Zorell.

Tobungus had been given to the twins by the Wood Frog Aramaltus as their first adventure started. Zorell joined them later after helping them battle a rogue fairy at the library. They were both helpful to the twins, but they seemed to hate each other. Sometimes their arguing was humorous, and sometimes it was distracting.

Just when the cat seemed ready to pounce, Derek said, "settle down, Zorell."

"Zorell?" Tobungus said. "Did he tell you his name was Zorell?"

"My name is Zorell," the cat hissed back.

"That's funny," Tobungus replied rubbing a finger across his spongy chin, "I spent the past four months thinking your name was NibbleBits." He raised his squirt bottle, expecting Zorell to lash out with his dagger-like claws.

Zorell took a deep breath and turned to Derek. "Do you see what I have had to put up with? The family I traveled with had a little girl who called me a lot of silly names, but my name is Zorell."

"Of course it is, precious widdle NibbleBits," Tobungus said.

"Tobungus," Derek warned, "that's enough. The next time I see you two fighting, I'm going straight to Iszarre."

The threat of the great wizard's disapproval was like a powerful magical spell. Tobungus and Zorell remained quiet as they entered the diner and found an open table for breakfast. Derek was happy to have them silent, while he watched the snake wizard Glabber place a stack of friddleberry pancakes in front of him.

When he was about to take his first bite of the pancakes, Deanna came down the worn wooden stairs and sat down in front of what she thought was her own food.

She looked down at a bowl of wiggling worms and orange leaves and jumped back in surprise. "Glabber," she shouted, "what *is* this?"

The sleek serpent wizard glided across the floor and rose up to the table. "Oops, sorry my dear," he hissed, "that was meant for my brother who is visiting from the Desert Realm."

"Your brother's here?" Derek asked, looking toward the large window behind the counter.

"Oh, yes," Glabber answered. "He's in the kitchen chasing his breakfast." As if on cue, a loud crash from breaking glasses came from the kitchen. "I'll be right back," Glabber said. "Oh, and I'll get you something a bit more to your liking." He grabbed the bowl and slithered away to get Deanna a plate of pancakes.

"It sounds like Glabber's brother is another Tobungus," Derek joked.

"Hmm?" Deanna said, a bit distracted. She was still grossed out from seeing the bowl of worms, and she was wondering where Derek had gone with the wand so quickly.

Before Deanna could ask Derek why he had run out of the room, Iszarre walked in through the diner's main door. Instead of his usual apron, the old wizard was wearing overalls and grimy boots. He was covered in dirt, and didn't look too happy.

"What happened to you?" Deanna asked.

"The magical armies are stirring," Iszarre said, sitting on a chair by the counter.

He flicked his wand toward the window to the kitchen, and a large mug of purple liquid floated to him. He took a long drink and sat back to relax. He offered no further explanation of his cryptic statement. Derek and Deanna simply looked at each other.

Glabber, the snake wizard, returned to their table and set a plate of pancakes in front of Deanna. He explained, "Every five hundred years, the seventeen magical armies rise from the underground catacombs. The armies join powerful wizards to decide who controls Elestra. The Army of the Ruby Dawn always follows the leaders of Magia, and Iszarre wanted to be sure that they are able to come to the surface. He's been digging near the old entrance to the catacombs since last night."

"Why wouldn't they have been able to come to the surface?" Derek asked.

"Iszarre heard a rumor that Eldrack was trying to put a spell over the catacombs' entrance to keep it closed," Glabber explained.

"A rumor?" Derek said.

"A prophecy, actually." Iszarre said. He hobbled over and sank into a chair next to Deanna. He picked up a pancake and mopped his sweaty forehead with it. Looking at the soaked pancake, he said, "I'll get this back to you after I clean it."

"No," Deanna said quickly, "you can keep it."

Iszarre looked surprised and thanked Deanna for the gift. He took another drink of the purple liquid and began to explain about the magical armies.

"Sometimes the armies follow the first powerful wizard who comes along," he said, "instead of waiting to see who the rightful leaders of each kingdom are. It is important to find the armies quickly so that they join us against Eldrack."

"Are you saying that there will be a war in Elestra?" Deanna asked nervously.

"Oh, no. It's not quite like that," Iszarre began. "It's more like a magical tournament. The armies battle each other with magical spells. When warriors are hit by spells, they simply return to the catacombs until the next battle. When one army wins the magical tournament, though, that army gives all of its magic to the wizard leading it. If Eldrack gets an army to follow him and they win, he will become even more powerful."

"I guess we better make sure that he doesn't win, then," Derek said grimly.

"But how does a wizard get a magical army to follow him?" Deanna asked.

"Some of the magical armies always follow the strongest wizards or paramages from one of the Six Kingdoms," Iszarre said. "Other armies are less predictable. You'll find that music is a powerful force in Elestra. Some armies are drawn to magical music. Eldrack may trick them into believing that he controls the source of music that they follow."

"So, if we find all of the moonstones and start all of the magical instruments, will that help us keep the armies on our side?" Derek asked.

"Oh, you will find that the music that will play after you return all of the moonstones to the arch will influence the armies," Iszarre said. "But, it will also help you in ways you cannot even imagine yet," he added with the smallest smile creasing his face. "But for now, you have another moonstone to find. If I recall correctly, you'll be going outside of Magia for the first time."

"Can't you tell us more?" Deanna asked, almost pleading. "We have so much to learn, and Eldrack already knows about all of this."

"Deanna, I have told you before that I can only tell you certain things," Iszarre said sympathetically. "You are learning a lot on your own, and you are becoming very powerful."

Deanna wanted to ask him more questions, but Derek interrupted her. He could tell that Iszarre had told them all that he would, and he wanted to solve the mystery of the ancient voice.

"Now that you're finally awake," Derek said, "we can get going to the library and find out where we need to go."

"Maybe I'm so tired because I stay up studying the Book of Spells," Deanna said quickly. She gathered her things and picked up her backpack. Before Derek could say anything, she got up and headed for the door.

Derek turned toward the door and whispered, "I study, Deanna. You'll find out."

# 2 Singing in the Rain

All morning, Derek had felt a growing sense of unease as he waited to head to the Library. The memory of the eerie voice echoed in his mind. He felt like it was hinting at something that they had to know if they were to be successful in Elestra. The continuing war between Tobungus and Zorell had added to his frustration, as did his sense that Deanna was moving especially slowly this morning.

Derek led the way toward the Library, with Deanna, Tobungus, and Zorell close behind. He looked back and saw Tobungus digging in his shoe bag. "What are you doing now?" he asked.

"Rain's coming," Tobungus said with his head buried deep in the floppy bag. He tried to pull his head out of the bag and explain, but he had gotten his head too far into the bag. He fought to free himself from the itchy burlap. After several minutes of struggling, he finally managed to slide the bag above his eyes. Much to Zorell's delight, it became stuck halfway up his spongy cap, making Tobungus look like he was wearing a bag of flour as a hat.

Tobungus saw Zorell laughing at his struggle. He spit a few threads of burlap that had caught on his tongue. "I'd rather not get a hairball," he said, giving the bag a final yank and freeing his mushroom cap head from the bag. "I'll leave that to NibbleBits."

A mighty hiss was followed by Zorell lunging at Tobungus. Deanna raised the Wand of Ondarell and shouted *"Deflecto."* A shimmering circular shield appeared between Zorell and Tobungus.

Zorell hit the shield and bounced backward. Before Tobungus could say anything, Zorell hissed again, "Next time, you may not be saved by a Guardian." He looked at Deanna and smiled warmly.

Deanna shook her head and slowly turned toward the giant fish laying in front of the fountain just down the block. "What on Earth?" she wondered.

"You mean what on Elestra?" Tobungus corrected, smiling at the enormous fish.

"Where do you suppose that odd fish came from?" she asked Derek. "Ugh, what a smell!"

Derek looked nervous as he said, "Well, you see, Deanna."

She cut him off. "You did this?"

"I had to stop another fight between these two," Derek replied, pointing at Tobungus and Zorell. "Only, I forgot how to, you know, get rid of the fish."

"Unbelievable," she said.

"Look, Deanna," Derek said, "I know that you're better with the wand. But, hey, I was able to think of a spell that I had read about to stop Tobungus' attack."

Deanna realized that Derek was feeling like he was not powerful enough, just like he had felt when they were in the Baroka Valley. Pointing the wand at the fish, she whispered, "*Reducio pisce*." The fish shrunk back to its normal size and floated into the fountain. "Now, what's this about rain?" she asked Tobungus, trying to change the subject.

"See for yourself," Tobungus answered. He pointed to a wall of rain a couple of blocks further down the street. The rain was so heavy that they could not even see the outlines of the buildings in that part of Amemnop. "That, dear Droopy, is a Magian superspout, and it's coming our way. Superspouts come three or four times a year and soak everything."

"My name's Deanna, Tobungus. Anyway, I guess we better hurry to the Library," she said. "I'm not sure how to get past something like that."

"Maybe I can help with that," Derek said. He grabbed the charm and opened the Book of Spells. "While I was studying," he began.

Deanna raised her eyebrows and was about to interrupt him, but he quickly continued, "Yes, I said studying. I came across the perfect spell."

He flipped through the pages until he found the Spell of the Magical Umbrella. He had seen it while waiting for Deanna to wake up earlier that morning. As he read the spell, he smiled to himself. "Okay, Deanna, to clear an area over your head, you have to say *Aquario Banishimento*. Got it?"

"Yeah, I think so," she replied.

Derek silently read the lines under the spell:

> *This spell requires seventh degree magic and should not be attempted by novice wizards. If the wizard does not possess strong enough magic, the spell will work in reverse – all of the rain from the superspout will fall directly on the wizard.*

He smiled to himself again, thinking that Deanna deserved an icy shower after delaying their start to the Library.

As they reached the edge of the downpour, Deanna raised the wand and took a deep breath. *"Aquario Banishimento."*

Derek waited for the rain to pour down on her, but instead, the sky began to clear.

*"Aquario Banishimento,"* she said more forcefully.

Derek thought he saw her eyes glow a bright green for a second. He looked up in amazement. It was as if giant hands were pulling the storm away. The skies cleared over Amemnop, and the sun came out to dry the city.

Several people looked out of windows and from under overhangs. One old woman murmured, "Can it be true? Is she the one?"

Deanna lowered the wand, turned, and hurried toward the Library, unsure what was so surprising about using a simple magical spell in a city filled with magical energy. Derek ran to keep up with her. Even Tobungus and Zorell forgot their argument, as they headed toward the Library.

The doors heading into the Library were fifteen feet tall and covered with intricate carvings of magical creatures. Once inside, they saw a sight that always amazed them. The bookshelves stretched five stories high. The walls were made of a dark brown wood, and the only windows were set near the ceiling.

Thousands of candles gave off tiny flickers of light that danced over the books, making them look like they were moving. The books weren't quite alive, but they were magical, and this sea of enchanted books made the library seem alive.

Deanna headed to the librarian's desk and quickly asked the book fairies to retrieve books about the Desert of the Crescent Dunes. The fairies had not had a large request in over a day and were anxious to stretch their wings. The swarm of insect-like fairies buzzed upward, pulling books from shelves near the ceiling.

Meanwhile, Tobungus and Zorell got back to trading insults. Being in the library stopped them from physically attacking each other, but they couldn't resist any chance to insult each other. Zorell's comments focused on Tobungus' musty aroma, while Tobungus' concentrated on the possibility that Zorell would cough up a flea-infested hairball on one of the books.

Derek was trying to ignore his two friends and the shrieks of the excited book fairies. He was still tired and cranky from waking up so early, so he closed his eyes. As his mind drifted away from the noises in the Library, a familiar, ancient voice said, *"Derek, the Archives."*

His eyes flew open. He looked around but saw only Deanna, Tobungus, and Zorell. They did not seem to hear the voice that was calling to him. He got up and walked toward the librarian's desk.

When he got to the librarian's desk, he closed his eyes. The soft voice returned. *"Derek, the Archives."*

"May I help you?" the tiny librarian asked.

"Um, I'm not sure," Derek began. "I'm looking for the Archives."

"Young man," the librarian replied sweetly, sweeping her hand across the Library, "this whole library is an archive."

"No, I mean, is there a special archive?" he asked.

"I'm sorry," the fairy replied a bit nervously this time, "but I don't know what you mean."

"Oh, I don't know," he thought back to his dream. "Does Gula Badu mean anything to you?" he asked hopefully.

The librarian looked around cautiously and then said in a hushed voice, "Follow me." She picked up a candle and motioned for Derek to follow her down a narrow aisle behind the large librarian's desk.

Together, they walked deeper into the mountainous book shelves. There were fewer candles in this part of the library, and shadows danced across the dark rows of books, making them seem even more alive.

After several minutes, they came to an ancient stone spiral staircase. They climbed down at least two hundred steps to a dark basement. The air became thicker as they descended deeper under the library. The walls were damp, and Derek thought that he heard water dripping somewhere in the distance.

The librarian fairy led Derek down a hallway that looked like a tunnel carved out of the rock under the Library. The tunnel reminded Derek of the Cave of Imprisonment, where his grandfather was being held. They walked for another ten minutes before they came to a large wooden door.

Derek heard the sound of running water somewhere nearby and asked, "Are we under the Fountain of the Six Kingdoms?"

The door creaked open. An ancient voice seemed to sneak out of the inner room, "No, we are under the River of Tranquility. Do not fear. Dark magic cannot penetrate the neutral water of the river."

Derek turned to ask the librarian a question, but a green haze floated above the ground where she had stood moments before. She had vanished in a puff of smoke. Turning back to the open door, he peered into the darkness and nervously said, "Who's there?"

A hooded figure shuffled slowly out of the room. Two wrinkled hands appeared from the brown sleeves of a long cloak and pulled the hood back. The oldest woman Derek had ever seen said, "Welcome to the Archive of Prophecies. I am Gula Badu."

# 3 The First Prophecy

Gula Badu looked like she had been carved from a tree that had survived centuries of stormy weather. The wrinkles lining her face reminded Derek of a tree's bark, and her eyes reminded him of gray driftwood.

Derek felt like his feet were glued to the rocky floor. Hearing the ancient voice made him feel like he had fallen into some sort of hole where time had stopped. Before he knew what was happening, the old woman floated into the corridor, gently grabbed him by the elbow, and guided him toward the doorway leading to the hidden Archives.

She looked at the nervousness filling his face and said, "Don't worry, Derek. There is something that you must see."

Her voice had a soothing tone. He felt a wave of contentment wash over his whole body. He took a deep breath to clear his mind and followed her into the room. He had never seen anything like this strange chamber. It was round, with wooden shelves lining the walls.

Instead of books, there were candles on the shelves, but none were lit. In the center of the room, a huge saucer-shaped disk held a fire of green flames.

"What is this place?" Derek asked in astonishment.

"This is the Archive of Prophecies," Gula Badu replied. "Very few people in Elestra know of its existence. You are the first visitor to the Archives in a very long time."

"But, why?" Derek began, but he could not think of anything else to say.

"Why, indeed," Gula Badu said. "I'll try to make this as simple as possible. You have heard of the Six Kingdoms of Elestra, no doubt."

Derek nodded and said, "Magia, the Ice Lands, the Sky Dragons or Dragon Realm, the Forest Kingdom, the Desert Realm, and Oceania."

Gula Badu smiled and said, "Very good! What no one has told you is that there is a Seventh Kingdom. The wizards from this forgotten land have a special power. While they do not possess the same magic that other wizards enjoy, they can see the future through the Green Flame."

"So, they're psychics?" Derek asked.

"Well, not exactly," Gula Badu answered. Her words came out like slow, thick syrup. "Hmm. How can I explain it? Magic is like a pulse of energy that started at the beginning of Elestra and continues into the future. It is timeless."

She walked closer to the green flames in the center of the room and motioned for Derek to follow her.

"When a wizard uses magic," Gula Badu continued, "he or she taps into that pulse and becomes one with all times—past and future. Wizards from the Six Kingdoms can use the magic, but they cannot see through time to the other points where the magic is used. Wizards from the Seventh Kingdom cannot use normal magic, but they can see through time. They use this power to write the History of Elestra."

"But if they see into the future, then how is that history?" Derek asked.

"A very good question. To these wizards, known as the Brotherhood of the Green Flame, there is no past or future. They see everything as a story which has already happened. The knowledge contained in their prophecies, however, can be dangerous if it falls into the wrong hands."

Derek understood that if a dark wizard knew how the forces of good were going to act, he could change his tactics. Derek immediately saw a problem with the Archives. "If these prophecies are so dangerous, then why aren't they destroyed?"

Gula Badu drew in a breath, wanting to avoid telling Derek too much. "The prophecies are protected by a powerful form of magic which prevents their destruction. While we cannot destroy the prophecies, we can keep them hidden."

"If they're supposed to stay hidden, why am I here?" Derek asked uncertainly.

"You are here because it takes a special type of magic to connect with the prophecies," Gula Badu explained. "When I called out, you were the one who heard me."

Derek liked the idea that he had some special magical power, but he was still confused. "But why did you call out to me?" he asked.

"We can only show the prophecies to wizards who are mentioned in the prophecies." She waited for Derek to realize what she was saying.

His eyes grew wide in surprise. Gula Badu reached to her right and pulled an unlit candle from its shelf. "This is the First Prophecy of the Great Struggle of Light. It is for you to read." She placed the candle on a small table in front of Derek.

"I don't understand," he said, looking at the large candle.

"When I light the candle, the words of the prophecy will flow from the tip of the flame." She placed a sheet of parchment paper on the table and casually waved a finger at the candle and said, "*Ignitio.*"

A flame on the candle's wick flickered at first and then burned brightly. Wax from the candle dripped down onto the paper. Derek squinted, and finally saw glowing words drifting from the flame. He whispered them as he read:

> *The Realms of Elestra will be torn asunder as the Five Hundred Year Battle nears. A rising tide of evil will imperil the land and endanger the rightful ruler. Through the mists of magical battle, two powerful wizards will emerge. They will complete many quests and fight many battles in the name of their King. They will take their places among Elestra's most powerful wizards, but they will struggle with a fateful decision. Following a terrible act of betrayal, the young wizards, first the sister, then the brother, will join their sworn enemy in the final battle.*

Derek was shaking as he finished reading the haunting passage. As he blinked from the intensity of the candle's flame, Gula Badu reached over and snuffed out the fire. She looked at the fear in his eyes, and said quietly, "Do not be afraid of your destiny, Derek."

"My destiny?" he blurted out. "What do you mean? To betray King Barado and help Eldrack? Eldrack kidnapped thirteen generations of my family. How could I ever join him?"

"Your family is very powerful, Derek," she said. She paused for a few seconds and seemed to choose her words carefully. "There are powerful reasons for you to fight against the evil that you sense is sneaking into the heart of Elestra. But, you and your sister have been dragged into this battle before you had received any magical training. As you complete your quests, you may choose to follow a different path. One that you think is right."

"My head hurts," Derek said, closing his eyes.

"I think that's enough for you today. It is time for you to rejoin your sister. But take this with you," Gula Badu said softly, handing him the parchment paper, which now held the words of the prophecy.

As Derek looked down at the paper in his hands, she said, "Show it to no one except your sister. If you wish to destroy it, you may do so."

She led him back to the staircase that rose to the Library far above. He ran up the stairs as quickly as he could and found Deanna finishing her research on their next adventure. She zipped her pack and asked the book fairies to return the final two books to their places on the shelves.

Deanna saw the worried look on Derek's face as he walked toward her. "What's wrong, Derek?" she asked.

He was still unsure about the meaning of the prophecy and did not want to worry her. "Hmm. Oh, nothing. I was just walking around by some of the stacks in back. I'm still a little tired from this morning. That's all." He knew that he looked like he was hiding something.

"Well, I've been working on our trip," she said, slightly annoyed that he seemed to have gone off exploring when there was work to be done. "We have to travel along the River of Tranquility to get to the Great Aquarian Divide which separates Magia from the Desert Realm. We can take a ferry across the Divide, so we should be there before dinner."

"You'll love the Desert Realm," Zorell purred. He looked at Tobungus and could hardly stop himself from laughing.

"I won't love it," Tobungus said with a disgusted look on his face. "Heat, sand, and worse," he whispered.

Deanna walked out of the Library, followed by Tobungus, Zorell, and finally Derek, who was still a bit shaken about the prophecy. "Hey, guys," Tobungus called. "Let's take drectaws along the river."

Deanna had no idea what he was talking about, but Zorell cut in, "For once, I have to agree with the slack-jawed fungal barnacle."

"Thank you so much, you walking advertisement for a flea dip," Tobungus shot back, moving closer to Deanna and out of Zorell's reach. "There's a stable near the east side of Amemnop by the river."

Derek needed to keep his mind off of the prophecy, so he let Tobungus and Zorell continue their bantering as they walked across town.

They walked down narrow streets that were lined with houses that looked like cylinders stacked on top of each other. Some of the houses were short and fat, and others reached high into the air.

The smell of food cooking in huge cauldrons escaped from the windows, and the sounds of the people inside made the twins feel like they were back home.

Soon, they left the rows of houses behind. They walked along the River of Tranquility and thought back to their relaxing gong ride on the river after they had left the Baroka Valley. Finally, they walked around a bend, and the stable Tobungus had described came into view. Deanna's jaw dropped. "What are those things?" she asked no one in particular.

Tobungus and Zorell looked at each other and seemed to agree to momentarily stop arguing. "Those are the drectaws," Tobungus replied. "They can be a bit tricky at first, but once you get used to the undulations, you'll enjoy the ride."

"Well, you may not enjoy the ride," Zorell said, "but it beats walking all the way to the Aquarian Divide."

The drectaws' elongated bodies looped up high off of the ground, with the top of the loop at least eight feet high. Dozens of pairs of legs covered the length of their bodies. As they moved, the legs on the section off of the ground retracted into the animal's torso. They looked like giant inchworms with the front and back ends of a horse.

Deanna walked over to the man who ran the stable and asked about renting four of the drectaws. As she reached for her bag of gold, he held up a hand, "Your service to Amemnop has already become legendary," he said. "I am honored to allow you and your fellow travelers to ride my drectaws." She smiled and thanked him, silently wondering about the honor they were about to experience.

As they rode along the River of Tranquility, Tobungus turned to Zorell and said, "One of these days, you'll have to do something to earn your keep. Just watch me for a while, and you might learn a thing or two."

"You know, Tobungus," Zorell said, "I've heard that mushrooms grow on manure. I was thinking that maybe you grew up on some steamy pile in a corner of that stable back there."

Derek laughed for the first time all day. He wondered whether these two really hated each other as much as they appeared to. He looked out over the river and understood how it had gotten its name. The surface was perfectly smooth. He could see reflections of the forests and mountains on the far side as if he were looking directly at them.

Looking at the river seemed to calm Derek and give him a sense of peace. He noticed that Tobungus and Zorell looked relaxed as well. The only thing that cut through his relaxation was the slow roller coaster ride that the drectaw was giving him.

Derek looked ahead and saw the river widening as it entered a huge lake. "Ah, we're almost there," Tobungus called out. "Just another ten minutes or so."

"Great," Deanna exclaimed as she passed them. Her drectaw didn't seem to like to take things "slow and steady." Derek laughed softly at the sight of her bouncing wildly in front of them.

The River of Tranquility was on the north side of Magia. On the horizon in the opposite direction, Derek could see a strip of large hills, or small mountains, running along the southern edge of the Magical Realm. One long mountain curled from the south and cut across Magia all the way to the lake.

Zorell saw Derek studying the mountain and said, "That is Mount Indecision in front of us. It is not only the highest mountain in Magia outside of the Bagayama Mountains, but it is also covered by challenges that make climbers wonder whether they really need to make it to the top."

"Magia circles all the way around Elestra," Derek noted. "Couldn't you just go in the opposite direction and get to the other side of the mountain?"

"It's not quite so simple, Derek," Zorell replied. "You can go in two directions to get to the same location, but once you are there, you find that you have reached different places."

"Huh?" Derek muttered.

"There are stories about a lost city just over the mountain that can't be reached if you travel around Magia to the west," Zorell answered mysteriously.

"Okay, listen," Derek said. "I can't keep all of these stories straight." After the prophecy and all of Iszarre's advice, his brain was beginning to feel overloaded. "We're not going to try to climb the mountain today, so just tell me if we can get into the part of the Great Aquarian Divide that will take us to the Desert Realm."

"We can sail to the Desert Realm up ahead, but we must be careful," Zorell purred. "The River of Tranquility has a twin, the River of Doubt. It runs along the southern border of Magia, and part of it flows along the mountain in front of us. It shoots out and creates great waterfalls in the middle of the lake."

"I don't see any waterfalls out there," Derek said.

"Elestra breathes very slowly," Tobungus said in response, as he pushed past Zorell to get closer to Derek.

"What does that mean?" Derek asked Zorell.

Zorell nudged the sides of his drectaw and looped past Tobungus so that he was next to Derek once again. "Tobungus is correct that Elestra breathes. A lot of the magic that wizards and other creatures use is wasted. It just floats around in the air. Plus, there's the magic that evaporates along with the waters of the rivers and streams. Elestra breathes this magic back in through the great ruby wells. It also breathes out the exhaust from making magic."

"Exhaust?" Derek said. "What, like some kind of smoke?"

"No, not smoke, Derek," Zorell purred. "It is energy, but this energy is completely without magic. Many interesting things happen when these bursts of energy explode from the surface. Keep your eyes open. One of the things you will see is that the River of Doubt is pushed along the streambed on the mountain ridge in front of us. That causes powerful waterfalls to fly out into the middle of the lake, but they don't last long."

"Believe me," Tobungus said, moving in between Derek and Zorell once more, "you don't want to get caught in a cloud of non-magical energy. You wouldn't be able to use your magic, and in Elestra, that can be a very bad thing."

"Can't you just leave the cloud?" Derek asked.

"Sometimes, yes, and sometimes, no," Tobungus chuckled.

Up ahead, they saw a small wooden pier with a small ferry tied up. A slightly round old man with very little hair stood up to greet them. He had a friendly smile and waved enthusiastically as they approached. Derek was relieved to see someone with a genuine smile.

Tobungus leaned over to Derek and said, "We have to watch out for this one. He's a devious little imp."

# 4 Don't Pay the Ferry Man

Derek leaned over toward Tobungus and whispered, "What do you mean, we have to watch out?"

Deanna hopped off of her drectaw and walked over to the ferry man. She threw her pack onto her back as she approached him.

"The ferry man is a Kadeelian Twister," Tobungus said. "I recognize him from an earlier trip I took." Tobungus, Derek, and Zorell climbed down from their drectaws, grabbed their packs, and started toward the dock.

"Kadeelian Twisters are shape-shifting sprites who take up normal jobs and are very friendly. . . at first," Tobungus continued. "They try to steal anything they can and then transform into tiny bolts of lightning. This one will try to get you to pay for the ferry ride before you leave. As soon as he has the money, he'll zip out of here."

Derek looked over and saw Deanna talking with the jolly old man. She was untying her bag of gold, preparing to pay for their ride. "Deanna," Derek shouted.

Deanna looked over, wondering what he wanted. "Wait a minute, Derek," she called. "I'm just taking care of our ride."

Derek jogged over to her side and gently pushed her bag aside. "Excuse me, sir, but it is custom where we are from to pay for a ferry ride after we reach the other side."

The little man looked at Derek with gleaming eyes. For the first time, Derek thought that his friendly appearance seemed fake. The man nodded his head and waved them onto the small ferry.

Derek and Tobungus boarded first, with Deanna and Zorell bringing up the rear. The ferry man held up a hand and said, "I'm sorry but the cat can't come on my boat."

"Ah," Zorell purred, "you're a Kadeelian."

"Why can't he come?" Deanna asked sharply.

"It's okay, Guardian Deanna," Zorell began, "Kadeelians and my species have a long standing disagreement. Perhaps it would be best for me to stay behind."

Derek was surprised to see Tobungus stand up quickly. "But, but, we are going to the Desert Realm," he sputtered. "Zorell may be particularly useful there."

Derek and Deanna could guess how much it must have hurt Tobungus to say that they needed Zorell. They knew it was important to bring the cat along.

Deanna looked around. She found a wooden plank, just large enough for Zorell to stand on and got a wonderful idea. "I hope you don't mind waterskiing," she said smiling.

"I don't know what waterskiing is," Zorell said, "but it doesn't sound like something that I'd enjoy."

"Nonsense," Tobungus laughed. "A little bath couldn't hurt. You can only lick so much dirt off of yourself."

"Unlike you, Toe-Gunkus, I like to clean myself," Zorell replied. "I suppose being moist and dirty is part of being a fungus."

"Alright, alright, you two," Deanna scolded. "It's time to get Zorell situated." She told Derek to position Zorell in the middle of the plank. Then, she raised the wand and uttered a string of spells that Derek could not follow. A shimmering golden rope connected the front of the plank to the wand. Zorell's feet glowed brightly for a second, and then Deanna said to the startled cat, "Try to lift your paws."

Zorell pulled as hard as he could, but he could not move his feet. They seemed to be glued to the wooden plank.

"That should do it," Deanna said smiling.

"All aboard!" Derek called. Deanna held the rope tightly as they climbed onto the ferry.

As the ferry pulled away from the shore, Deanna towed the miniature raft behind them.

Zorell looked terrified of falling into the water, but Deanna called out that she would keep him upright until they reached the other side. True to her word, she navigated Zorell safely through bubbling rapids, around rocks, and over water plants.

Several times along the way, the ferry man asked if they would pay him, but Derek politely refused each time. As soon as they reached the far side of the Great Aquarian Divide, Derek reached into the bag of gold and handed the ferry man three large coins.

Once he had the money, the ferry man spun into a tiny tornado and shot into the sky like a bolt of lightning.

"I guess you were right," Derek said to Tobungus. Tobungus simply nodded.

Deanna reeled in Zorell who mumbled something about feeling like a fish. Once he was on dry land, they all heard a noise and looked back across the water. A huge jet of water shot from the River of Doubt on Mount Indecision and splashed down into the Aquarian Divide.

"I'm glad we're not out there now," Deanna said.

"That would have been bad," Tobungus said seriously, shuddering at the thought of getting caught in a magicless waterfall.

The four turned away from the water and set out on a sandy path into the Desert Realm. The oppressive heat was the first thing to greet them as they climbed a dune at the water's edge.

From the top of the sandy hill, they could see a small village with tan buildings crafted of rough stone. Heat seemed to be rising from every surface and the air shimmered. Massive swarms of insects rose above the streets, only to be scooped up by giant bat-like birds which flew in figure eight patterns over the town.

Derek's and Deanna's feet sank into the warm sand as they ran down the dune, but they made it to the bottom without any real trouble. They walked up one street and down another, without seeing anyone.

"I wonder if the town is abandoned," Derek asked.

"Or worse, it could be a ghost town," Deanna replied softly.

Zorell stopped, the hair on his back standing up. He let out a soft noise, somewhere between "shh" and a hiss.

"What is it, Zorell?" Deanna asked.

Zorell's eyes narrowed, and he whispered, "There's someone watching us from the shadows in that window ahead."

Derek saw a large opening in the square building in front of them. There was no light inside, and the sun was behind the building, so everything and everyone inside was in shadow. "Who's there?" Derek asked boldly.

At first, nothing happened. Then, a rustling sound confirmed that Zorell had been right. Finally, a girl with black hair, nervously peered around the opening. "Do you bring the beasts?" the girl asked.

Derek looked at Tobungus and Zorell, and said, "These two are beastly, but no, they are not beasts." He waited for a reply that never came. Sensing that his attempt at a joke had failed, he asked, "Who are you?"

The girl eased closer to the window. "My name is Dahlia," she said. "If you are not working with the beasts, then why have you come to Roparcia during such a terrible time?"

"We are travelers unaware of any trouble," Deanna replied. "We didn't even know this place was called Roparcia. We are on a quest to fight against an evil wizard who is trying to take control of Elestra."

Dahlia stared at Deanna for several seconds, and finally let a smile spread across her face. "Come in, and we can talk about your quest and the beasts that terrorize my people."

Derek followed Deanna into the stone house. Tobungus and Zorell trailed behind. The inside was surprisingly bright, with colorful furniture, rugs, and lamps of glowing liquid lining the walls. Tobungus went to a dark corner which was a bit cooler than the rest of the room. Zorell paced around the room, listening for any sounds from outside.

Dahlia walked over to the window and closed the colorful, shining curtains. Then, she turned to a large cage filled with foot-long lizards munching on ripe berries. "Do you want a lizard tail?" the girl asked.

"What?" Deanna answered, not knowing if Dahlia was kidding.

Dahlia reached into the cage, grabbed one of the lizards and ripped its tail off. The lizard simply climbed back onto its perch and began eating again. Dahlia wiped the tail off, and began chewing on it.

Deanna's eyes grew wide, and her mouth hung open. Derek shook his head to make sure he was seeing clearly.

She saw the looks of horror on Derek's and Deanna's faces. "Don't worry," she laughed, "these are sugar lizards. They eat the sweet berries and concentrate the sugars in their tails. The tails naturally break off and can be eaten. The lizard will grow a new tail in a day or two." She reached in and grabbed two more tails, and handed them to Derek and Deanna.

Derek built up his courage and took a large bite and was surprised to find that the tail tasted like a huge jelly bean. He took another bite and said, "Deanna, this is really good. You have to try it."

She nervously took a bite, temporarily forgetting about their quest. "So," Dahlia said, "you are on a quest. I am sorry for not inviting you in right away, but with the beasts roaming our lands, we cannot be too sure about visitors."

"What's the story with these beasts?" Derek asked, while using his tongue to dig out chunks of the jelly-like lizard tail from his teeth.

Dahlia sank into a floppy chair. Derek and Deanna chose chairs near Dahlia and sat down. "The beasts must have heard the Legend of the Desert Treasure," Dahlia said. "They have come and raided every village, every museum, and every temple."

"That's horrible," Deanna said.

"Luckily, they have not taken anything yet," Dahlia said. "They have even left the Golden Scrolls of Roparcia, one of my people's most valuable collections."

"If they're not taking anything, they must be looking for something. But, what are they looking for?" Derek asked.

"The Legend says that the treasure is an item of unimaginable value, a single jewel," Dahlia sighed. "The problem is that no one knows where it is or what it looks like."

"We know what it looks like," Deanna said softly, glancing over at Derek. Dahlia looked at her in surprise. "And," she continued, "we know who has sent the beasts to Roparcia."

# 5 The Crying Arch

"Eldrack has a head start," Derek said, looking out the window.

"Who's Eldrack?" Dahlia asked. A wave of fear crossed her face.

"Eldrack," Deanna began, "is a dark wizard. No, actually, he is THE dark wizard. He's trying to find the moonstones which will help him become more powerful.

"And it sounds like the single jewel you described could be the third moonstone," Derek added. "We are searching for the moonstones, trying to find them before Eldrack does. When we find them, we take them to Amemnop where they can be protected."

"Dahlia," Derek said, "you don't know us, but you have to trust us. We need to know where the treasure is. If the beasts get there first, everyone in Elestra may suffer."

"I have seen the beasts," Dahlia said, recalling the frightening experience. "You are much better than those monsters, so I will help you any way I can." She thought back to the legends she had heard. "The treasure is supposed to be hidden in a temple in the Desert of the Crescent Dunes."

"The Desert of the Crescent Dunes. How do we get there?" Deanna asked.

Dahlia walked over to a ten-foot tall tapestry hanging on the wall opposite the window. "Help me turn this over," she said to Derek.

The side of the tapestry that had been facing the wall was covered with pictures of creatures and buildings all depicted in bright, rich colors. Around the edges were symbols that Derek recognized as hieroglyphs.

"Where did you get this tapestry?" Deanna asked in amazement as she walked over to take a closer look.

Dahlia smiled, but did not answer. Instead, she ran her finger along the row of symbols, and they began to glow with an eerie light. After a few moments, she found the important passage she was looking for:

*The Desert of the Crescent Dunes is a magical area to the northeast. You can search for years and never find the Desert. To successfully enter the desert, you must first find the Arch of the Dune's Tear. Once you walk through the Arch, you will see the Desert of the Crescent Dunes stretching out before you, and you will see a pyramid reaching toward the clouds.*

"How will we find the Arch of the Dune's Tear?" Deanna asked.

"That's a good question," Dahlia answered, frowning in thought. "The carpet does not explain that, but it does say that if you enter the wrong arch, you will be sent to an underground labyrinth that will take years to escape."

"Great," Derek said. "Anything else we should know?"

"Well," Dahlia said, tracing her finger over a line of hieroglyphs lower on the tapestry, "there is one thing. When you get near the Sea of Arches, the desert spring snakes will pop out of the sands and try to bite you. The bad news is they're poisonous. Actually, they're very poisonous."

"Any good news?" Tobungus asked sarcastically.

"Actually yes," said Dahlia, turning to Tobungus with a smile. "The spring snakes are almost totally blind. They sense vibrations and will attack areas with a lot of movement, so you can trick them."

Deanna stood up, "Well, we'd better get going. Eldrack's beasts already have a head start, and Dahlia has given us all the information she can."

"We have a good place to continue our search," Derek nodded.

They pulled hats from their packs and slathered their arms and noses with the last of the sunscreen that they usually carried for hikes on sunny days. Tobungus sprayed a musty smelling liquid all over himself to stay moist in the sun.

Dahlia gave them a pack with sandwiches, water jugs, and lizard tails for their journey through the desert. They thanked her for the food and information and headed back into the sun-drenched desert.

They had only gone a few steps before Tobungus stopped and said, "Wait, I need a new pair of shoes for the desert." He rooted around in his shoe bag for two or three minutes and shook the bag in frustration.

"What's the matter, Tobungus?" Derek asked. "Don't you have shoes for the desert?"

"Why would I have shoes for the desert?" Tobungus snapped. "This place is miserable already. I'm a mushroom. I can't take the heat. And, there's no moisture. A hot rainforest at least has humidity."

"Well, we don't have all day," Deanna said. "You must have something you can wear."

"I do have one idea," Tobungus replied. He pulled a pair of snowshoes out of the bag and snapped them over his regular shoes. "Sand is just like snow, only hot and disgusting, right?" he added.

"I can't wait to see how this works out," Derek whispered to Deanna.

Zorell rolled his eyes and led them out of the village.

Before long, it was clear that snowshoes were not meant for sand. Tobungus had gotten stuck at least eight times. He finally ripped the snowshoes off and threw them off of the dune where they were standing.

"Ah!" he yelled, realizing that he had just chucked a pair of his beloved shoes further into the desert.

"Don't worry," Deanna said. She pulled out the wand, pointed it at the snowshoes which were lying about fifty feet away, and said, "*Retrievus.*"

The snowshoes shook in the sand and then flew to Deanna. She carried them over to Tobungus and suggested, "Hiking boots, perhaps?"

Tobungus wiped the sand off of the snowshoes and put them back in the shoe bag. From then on, he trudged through the sand in hiking boots, grumbling as he went.

After two hours of hiking through the heat, the dune-covered horizon became dotted with huge stone arches. As they got closer, they saw at least forty arches. They realized that it was not going to be easy to determine which one led to the magical Desert of the Crescent Dunes.

Zorell had quietly taken the lead, but stopped suddenly. His fur stood on end, and he jumped backwards just as a six-foot snake coiled like a spring shot up from under the sand. The snake rose thirty feet into the air and then settled back into the soft sand.

Deanna told everyone to stop right where they were so that she could look through the Book of Spells. She remembered Dahlia's hint that the snakes could be fooled by vibrations.

Finally, she drew the wand and pointed it at the sand. She used the *Spell of Dancing Dirt* to make the sands dance to her right. Immediately, another spring snake shot up from under the dancing sands. She continued to use the spell to trick the snakes as they walked along.

Derek quickly identified a problem with their strategy, however. They were so focused on the snakes that they were not able to focus on the arches. But, they didn't dare take their eyes off of the snakes and try to figure out which arch was the right one.

After Derek had been watching the snakes for a while, he noticed that their heads were pointing forward, and a large part of their body was coiled behind them. "Deanna," he called, "hold off on that spell for a minute."

She looked surprised, but lowered the wand. Derek walked forward, stomping on the sand as he went. He stopped, stomped in place, and waited. He felt the sand move slightly and jumped backward, but only by about a foot. When the spring snake came to the surface, Derek was standing on its coiled back. The snake rose into the air, with Derek along for the ride.

Derek quickly looked around and saw that off to their left, two dunes were shaped like closed eyes. One of the dunes had an arch just below it, making it look like a tear coming out of the eye. His feeling of triumph was short lived, however.

At that moment, he realized that he had not thought about the trip back to the surface. He was nearly thirty feet above the ground and falling fast. Just before he hit the sand, he stopped. It felt like a silky net had caught him. He looked over and saw Deanna pointing the wand in his direction.

"Thanks, Deanna," he said, as he turned toward the dunes he had seen.

"That was a pretty stupid move," Deanna called, hurrying over to catch up with him. Tobungus and Zorell followed close behind her.

"Not so fast," Derek replied smiling. "I wanted to see the area from above, and I've found the arch."

"Well, where is it?" Tobungus shouted.

"It's over that way," Derek said, pointing to a pair of arches to their left. "I think we can outrun the snakes if we all stick together."

As they sprinted over the sandy desert floor, dozens of spring snakes shot into the air behind them. Deanna continued to fire off the *Spell of the Dancing Dirt* as they ran.

When they reached the arch that Derek had seen, Deanna used the spell again and watched as a pack of snakes that had been following them shot skyward.

"How can you be sure that this is the right arch?" Deanna asked.

Pointing to the two eye-shaped dunes, Derek explained, "From above, those two dunes look like eyes. This arch looks like a tear coming from one of the eyes."

"You're sure about this?" Deanna asked uncertainly. "There's nothing on the other side of the arch. No pyramid. Nothing."

"No, I'm not sure," Derek said, "but this is Elestra. The arch must be magical."

Deanna was about to argue, when she felt the ground beneath their feet began to rumble again.

Thinking that he'd rather take his chances with the arch than with the snakes, Derek grabbed Deanna's hand and pulled her toward the arch. Tobungus and Zorell followed quickly behind.

Walking through the arch felt like walking through a solid curtain of water from a waterfall. Once through the arch, they saw a pyramid rising toward the clouds. There were fifty foot statues of cat-like creatures lining the pathway to the pyramid's only visible door.

"Now those are decorations I could get used to," Zorell said loudly to Tobungus.

"Great, we've come to the Hairball Hall of Fame," Tobungus muttered, shaking his head.

# 6 The Cat's Meow

Derek and Deanna looked more closely at the statues, and both thought that the huge cats looked very much like Zorell. They looked back and saw their furry friend happily swishing his tail as he nuzzled against one of the stone cats' huge paws.

Deanna rushed to the wide stone stairs that led into the temple, but Derek lagged behind. He kept looking back toward the Arch. "What's wrong, Derek?" Deanna asked.

"I'm not sure," he answered. "I feel like someone's following us."

Deanna immediately drew the wand, expecting an attack from Eldrack. She tiptoed slowly back toward Derek who was looking at her like she was crazy. "What?" she whispered angrily.

"You do realize that you're tiptoeing on sand, don't you?" he shot back, trying to keep from laughing. His expression changed when he saw Deanna staring at something behind him. He whirled around just as a small figure jumped out from behind one of the cat statues.

"Wait," he yelled, just before Deanna let a spell loose from the wand. "Dahlia," Derek said, "What are you doing here?"

"I decided I wanted to help you," Dahlia said. "I know the Desert Realm better than you do. I thought you could use my help."

"Fine," Deanna said, slowly lowering the wand, "Just don't scare us like that anymore."

Derek felt the hair on his neck rise. He looked all around him and saw the sand moving. "Deanna, we've got a problem."

As if in response to his words, a small sand tornado sprang out of the sand to their left. As it approached, a vine-like tentacle with suction cups underneath reached out toward them.

"*Cyclonicus,*" Deanna shouted, pointing the wand at the strange creature. The mini-tornado began bouncing up and down along the desert floor. At least a dozen tentacles danced wildly from the sand, then disappeared.

"You defeated a sand beast!" Dahlia cheered.

"Not so fast," Deanna replied. She was looking nervously at areas where it looked like the sand had begun to boil. Soon, seven more sand beasts had appeared. She knew that she could never perform enough spells to defeat the growing army of beasts.

"Get up the stairs!" Tobungus yelled as he ran past them. "We have to get the sand beasts out of the sand."

Not stopping to ask why having sand beasts out of the sand was better than having them in the sand, Derek, Deanna, Dahlia, and Zorell followed Tobungus up the stairs. The sand beasts left their sand tornadoes behind and wiggled their way up the stairs. Hundreds of slashing tentacles swiped at the children's feet.

Suddenly, an enormous shadow moved across the wall of the pyramid. Derek looked up and saw a giant bird that looked like a pelican with a floppy pouch under its beak. He guessed that the bird was the size of a small airplane. As it circled overhead, its huge mouth opened, and dozens of smaller versions of itself flew out. The smaller birds dove at Derek and the others. Their razor sharp beaks moved from side to side.

"Knifebirds!" Dahlia called out. "Stay away from their beaks. They can slice through solid rock."

"Great, Tobungus," Deanna shouted. "The sand beasts may be slower out of the sand, but now they've got these birds to help them." She saw that Derek was further up the stairs and called out to get his attention.

"It's no good going this way!" Derek yelled back to Deanna.

Deanna saw the attacking birds swooping toward them and turned back to the sandy surface. When the knifebirds appeared, the sand beasts jumped back into the sand. Even though the sand beasts were once again in their tornadoes where they were more dangerous, the bottom stairs were clear. With the birds following them, Derek, Deanna, and Dahlia ran back down the stairs and dove behind one of the huge statues.

Derek and Deanna ducked down, waiting to be attacked by the vicious birds, but nothing happened. They could still hear the whizzing sound of spinning sand, but none of the attackers came to them. Derek peeked out and saw that hundreds of sand beasts and knife birds had surrounded them but stood silently twenty feet from the statue.

"What's going on?" Deanna whispered. Derek shook his head slightly. She could see from his expression that Derek had no answers.

"Oh, no," Tobungus moaned off to their right. He had his hand over his eyes and was shaking his head. "I can't believe this is happening."

Deanna was worried about her friend and said softly, "Don't worry, Tobungus, we'll think of something."

"Too late," Tobungus replied. He pointed to the next statue where Zorell had appeared.

Deanna looked at Zorell and saw that he seemed to be doing some sort of dance. His head and tail swished from side to side. He waved his paws in the air with his long claws exposed. He hissed at a group of sand beasts through bared teeth. The sand beasts in that direction scattered.

"I'm not seeing this," Tobungus lamented. "This is misery piled on top of indignity. Deanna, I can't bear to watch. Please use a spell to put me to sleep until this is over."

Deanna ignored Tobungus' ranting and instead focused on the Book of Spells. She had a plan, but needed the right spell. She found the *Spell of the Storm's Breath* and quickly memorized the words she would need.

Zorell was busily hissing half of the sand beasts and knife birds back toward the arch they had used to come to the temple.

"Zorell!" Deanna shouted. "I have an idea. Try to move that group off to the left toward that other arch."

Zorell saw the arch she was pointing to and moved to his right. He turned and hissed again, shepherding the creatures toward the target arch. When they were arranged in front of the arch, Deanna yelled, "*Dragonia Gustahr*."

A strange sound filled the air. It was as if the sky took a deep breath and blew a storm directly at the sand beasts and knifebirds. The wind carried the attackers through the arch where they disappeared.

"They can wander the labyrinth for a while," Deanna shouted over the howling wind.

Zorell and Deanna worked together to send the other beasts and birds through nearby arches. Before long, it was over, and Tobungus sobbed in disgust at the display that Zorell had put on.

"Where did you learn that dance?" Tobungus asked. "Wait, I know. It was at a meeting of the flea and mange fan club."

"If you're really nice to me, I'll teach you the dance after we return to Amemnop," Zorell purred to Tobungus as he passed him on the stairs to the pyramid's entrance.

"I'd rather kiss one of the stink pigs of Revollar, but thanks anyway," Tobungus shot back.

"Do I want to know what a stink pig is?" Derek asked.

"The name pretty much says it all," Zorell answered. "Although, I think there may be a lot of types of fungus growing in the Revollarian pig pens," he added slyly.

"Go chase your tail, fleabag," Tobungus said.

"Time to cool it," Derek said, quickly walking between them. "We need to go into the temple and get the third moonstone before Eldrack gets here."

Zorell and Tobungus nodded to yet another temporary truce and followed Derek, Deanna, and Dahlia into the temple.

# 7 Eye on the Prize

There was no door to the pyramid temple. Instead, a narrow opening in the stone allowed visitors inside. The doorway blocked light from outside, so the passageway was pitch black.

"You better find a spell to light things up," Derek said to Deanna.

"No, I can take care of this," Dahlia said. Almost instantly, the passage was bathed in a bright yellow glow. Derek saw that Dahlia was holding a small glass jar on a string. Inside the jar were tiny caterpillars that gave off yellow flashes.

With the passage bathed in caterpillar flashes, Derek led the way deeper into the pyramid. "Does it seem like we're going up?" he asked the others.

Tobungus bent over. "We're definitely heading toward the top of the pyramid," he said between deep breaths.

Ahead, the tunnel turned off to the left. After several more minutes, it turned left again. They realized that they were spiraling upward along the outer walls of the pyramid. Finally, the tunnel ended at a doorway covered by a gauzy curtain.

Light filtered out from the doorway, so Dahlia slid the caterpillar jar back into her bag. Deanna pushed the curtain aside and walked into a large room with a high ceiling that rose to a point in the center. They were directly under the tip of the pyramid now.

The light in the room came from circular windows on the north and south walls. The west wall had no windows, but was covered by a huge dusty mural and hieroglyphs.

There were small cat statues along the walls and a large statue of a cat looking upward on the west side of the room. "It just keeps getting worse," Tobungus muttered.

Zorell purred and rubbed up against the large statue. "This is paradise," he mewed to Tobungus. "I know it's not the cozy dank, moist cellar you would like, Tobungus, but you should feel good seeing these heroic statues."

"Heroic?" Tobungus sputtered. "I'm surrounded by statues of King Hairball and his Ministers of Manginess. Not to mention that I haven't recovered from watching you do the itchy flea dance."

"Sorry to correct you, Mushpot, but it's the Dance of the Golden Talons. It's beautiful. Noble really. Don't you think?" Zorell added proudly.

"What I think is that the sand beasts were afraid that you were going to shake fleas on them," Tobungus answered.

Derek and Deanna were trying to ignore Tobungus and Zorell as they searched the statues for the moonstone. They came together near the west wall and looked up at the dust-covered mural. It was hard to make out exactly what was in the painted scene.

Derek began wiping the dust and sand off of the picture. Soon, they could see a group of people standing around the base of a statue of a woman, but they could not yet tell what she was doing.

Deanna looked away from the mural and saw a life-size statue of a woman near the middle of the room. The statue was facing the image of the moon in the mural, and the woman had a very serious look on her face. She was holding a scroll in one hand and something that looked like a necklace in the other hand.

Deanna studied the statue for several minutes, but couldn't find any clues to the moonstone's location.

Dahlia was wiping off the hieroglyphs on the mural and started to read:

*The Great Guardian entered the desert with the treasure of the moon. Before his fall, at the break of day, he hid the treasure opposite the sun.*

As Deanna listened to Dahlia, she looked at the small windows in the ceiling. She counted fourteen windows—seven on the north wall and seven on the south wall. She had an idea, but was confused because there were fifteen moons, but only fourteen windows. Then, she thought of the words, *"at the break of day, he hid the treasure opposite the sun."*

The sun rose in the east. The mural had been painted on the wall opposite the rising sun. Deanna turned around, and her eyes quickly scanned the east wall. "Derek, look!" She pointed at a single window near the top of the wall.

When Derek didn't respond, Deanna looked over and saw that he had just finished uncovering the entire scene. The statue of the woman in the mural was looking up at the moon. Rays of sunlight shimmered off of the moon in the mural.

"It must be the moonstone," Tobungus shouted. They all looked at the shimmering image of the moon, and Derek climbed up on a statue to wipe the dust away, hoping that years of sandy winds had covered the stone.

But, Derek found nothing but the rock that made up the rest of the walls. There was no moonstone hidden under the layers of dust. Searching for the answer he felt was right in front of him, he turned to examine the window Deanna had discovered.

"Deanna," Derek said, "Dahlia said that the stone was hidden at the break of day. The sun probably shines through that one window when it rises, but it's afternoon now. We can't see what sunlight shining through that window would look like."

"Leave that to me," Deanna said. She opened the *Book of Spells* and found the spell she needed. She pulled out the wand, pointed it at the single window and said, *"Helios luminari."* The window lit up and a beam of light like the rising sun came through the window and struck the mural. The light hit the moon in the picture.

The kids noticed that tiny, crushed gems had been pushed into one of the rays of moonlight that were carved in the mural. The tiny stones lit up and created a beam of light.

Derek, Deanna, and Dahlia followed the light away from the moon. Across the mural, the beam of light led to a picture of a dragon that stood before two people.

Deanna and Derek started dusting the dragon off. Soon, they uncovered a shining jewel that hung around the dragon's neck. Derek reached out and took the yellow moonstone from the necklace that had been carved into the wall. He turned toward Tobungus excitedly but was surprised to see Tobungus still staring at the dragon painted on the wall.

"The purple dragon," Tobungus said quietly.

"Yes," Zorell replied, coming to stand by his side. "Could Eldrack have captured the Purple Dragons at the same time he imprisoned Gelladrell?"

"No one has seen the Purple Dragons since the Red Dragon King was defeated," Tobungus said.

Derek and Deanna always worried when Tobungus and Zorell talked to each other without arguing. "What's going on, guys?" Derek asked, lowering his hand that held the jewel.

"The mural shows a dragon wizard here in the Desert Realm," Tobungus said.

"Why is it so unusual to see a dragon pictured in the Desert Realm?" Deanna asked.

"A group of dragon wizards disappeared hundreds of years ago when the King of the Dragon Realms was attacked," Zorell answered grimly.

"We'd have to check," Tobungus said, "but that attack was probably around the same time that Gelladrell came here to hide the moonstone." They all stood quietly in thought, not sure what to make of the presence of purple dragons in the mural.

Deanna's attention shifted to the statue of the woman looking at the moon. Her face had changed. She was smiling. Deanna moved closer and saw the statue move slightly.

Light started to shine from inside the statue. It grew stronger, and then a strong wind swirled around the room. The woman in the statue closed her eyes and said, "Whew, am I glad to be out of there." She stepped off of the pedestal and put her hand on Deanna's shoulder.

"But, you're a statue," Deanna stammered.

"So was Grandpa," Derek reminded her.

"Deanna, Derek, I am a member of the Sisterhood of the Ruby Dawn," she said happily. "And, I have a couple of things for you." She handed Derek the scroll and said, "That is the Lost Scroll of Roparcia." She looked over at Dahlia and said, "The scroll was meant for Derek. I'm sure that he will take care of it." Dahlia just nodded, with her mouth hanging open in surprise.

"Why me?" Derek asked, preparing to unroll the scroll.

"No, don't open it here," the woman said. "Wait until you are back in Magia. Study the scroll when you are alone." She brushed the hair out of Derek's eyes and said, *"Why you*? It's for you because you are one of the two Mystical Guardians who will bring peace to Elestra, and because you are the one who can hear the thoughts of the seers. Gula Badu has spoken to you with her mind, and you have heard her. That is a rare gift, Derek."

"Gula Badu?" Deanna said.

"It's a long story," Derek replied. "She guards the Archive of Prophecies. I'll tell you about it later."

The woman turned back to Deanna. "And for you, I have something that you must protect with all of your magic." She placed the necklace which had a deep red jewel on a chain of almost pure white metal around Deanna's neck. "This amulet must be delivered to Iszarre. He will know what to do with it."

Deanna rubbed the smooth surface of the jewel. It felt hot against her fingers and seemed to vibrate slightly.

"Can you tell us anything to help us with our quest?" Derek asked quickly.

"No," the woman answered. "I cannot tell you anything because I have seen the prophecies, and if I tell you about them, the prophecies will be broken, and a wave of magic will wash across the land against you. But then, you are already starting to learn about prophecies and how they can change. I must not say any more."

Before Derek or Deanna could say anything else, the woman flicked her wand toward the pedestal where she had been standing and a new statue appeared. Derek laughed out loud. The statue showed Tobungus and Zorell together, looking like the best of friends.

"Outrageous," Tobungus shrieked.

"Insulting," Zorell added.

"Perhaps the statue is another prophecy," the woman said playfully. She nodded respectfully at Dahlia, flicked her wand a final time, and disappeared in a cloud of dust.

Derek gave the moonstone to Deanna and led the way quickly out of the pyramid. When they reached the exit, they slowed down. They expected a new wave of sand beasts and knife birds to be waiting for them. Instead, the desert was calm and there were no noises, other than the gentle whistling of the wind.

They ran down the steps to the row of giant cat statues. "Don't you want to stay a little longer?" Zorell teased Tobungus.

"The sooner I get out of this nightmare, the better," Tobungus answered.

As they reached the arch, Deanna said, "It looks like we beat Eldrack to this moonstone. Maybe we can get back to Amemnop without any problems."

Derek nodded. He liked the idea of avoiding Eldrack. He sighed in relief and led the group through the arch.

# 8 Surrendering the Treasure

As he walked back through the arch, Derek felt the same sensation of walking through a waterfall. He shook his head to get rid of the odd feeling. When he opened his eyes, he sensed that returning from the desert wasn't going to be as easy as he had hoped. He saw that the sky had turned dark gray and was dotted with clouds that seemed to be boiling. Lightning streaked across the sky and thunder rolled.

"Uh oh," Tobungus whispered behind Derek. "It looks like our old friend was waiting for us."

On top of the next dune, Eldrack stood with his black cape flowing in the howling wind. Hundreds of sand beasts surrounded him. Three giant knifebirds circled overhead, waiting to release swarms of the smaller birds from their neck pouches.

"Deanna," Eldrack roared, "Give me the moonstone."

"You're always a step too late," Deanna replied bravely. "The moonstone will help protect Elestra from your evil power."

"You don't know anything about evil power," Eldrack hissed. He raised his wand and shot a fiery ball of magical energy that hit the sand ten feet to Deanna's right. Before she could react, three more fireballs sent sand flying at her feet.

Deanna jumped out of the way of the fiery blasts. She was ready to use a spell to freeze Eldrack's next fireball, when she heard a noise to her right.

A wave of sand beasts was moving up the dune where Deanna stood. She raised her wand and shouted, *"Hydrolus."* A jet of water shot from her wand and soaked the sand around the sand beasts. She then yelled, *"Hydro Fridgin."* The water froze into a thick sheet of ice. Some of the sand beasts were trapped under the ice, and some had their tentacles frozen in the ice.

The desert heat quickly started melting the ice. At the same time, a group of knifebirds began to dive toward Deanna. She saw that the ice had completely melted, so she pointed the wand at it again and said, *"Precipitato Magicum."* The water shot up into the air. She quickly shouted, *"Hydro Fridgin,"* and the curtain of water froze into an ice wall just before the knifebirds reached it. The huge birds crashed into the ice and fell to the ground stunned.

Eldrack had been silently watching Deanna's burst of magical spells. When he saw the knifebirds fall to the soggy sands of the desert, he shouted, "Deanna, I can't let you continue to attack my friends." He fired a blast of hot air that instantly melted the ice wall.

Deanna was thinking furiously, trying to come up with some spell that she could use to stop Eldrack. She tried the *Cyclonicus* spell to suck him into the ground, but he was too far away and her spell missed. Instead, a small tornado of sand ten feet to Eldrack's right spun and disappeared into the ground.

Deanna saw blobs of sand melting into glass where Eldrack had sent his spells. "You must give me the moonstone!" he bellowed.

Deanna thought about the melting sand and came up with an idea. Derek and the others were slowly moving between dunes, hoping that Eldrack would not notice them. Derek looked back and saw that Deanna had stopped. She was kneeling down, pointing her wand at the sand. "Come on, Deanna," he shouted.

Eldrack heard Derek's call and turned his attention away from Deanna. "Run!" Tobungus yelled to Derek and Dahlia.

Before they could move, Eldrack raised his wand and created a curtain of fire behind them. "Stay right where you are," he said calmly. He turned back to Deanna and said, "Deanna, it's up to you. Shall I take your friends or the moonstone?"

"Okay," Deanna shouted, "you can have the moonstone, but you have to promise to let us all go."

"Fine. I promise to let you go," Eldrack replied. "Just give me the moonstone."

"Don't trust him, Deanna," Tobungus yelled.

"Tobungus is right," Zorell said. "He'll get the moonstone and still capture us."

"We can be sure that he won't," Deanna said. "Eldrack, I'll give you the stone if you use the *Oriolix* Charm."

"I don't think I know that one," Eldrack hissed.

"The *Oriolix* Charm makes a promise unbreakable," Deanna said. She opened the Book of Spells and read the words to him, *"Oriolix bantu flan tabu."*

Eldrack took a deep breath and repeated the words. "Now, give me the moonstone," he said between clenched teeth. As she pulled the stone out, he said, "You're showing too much caring for your friends. Iszarre will not be happy."

"Iszarre will know that I am doing the right thing," Deanna said. She pulled the yellow stone out and said, "Just to be sure, you can go fetch the stone." She tossed the stone in the air and pointed the wand at it. *"Airio,"* she shouted. The moonstone flew over the dunes and out of sight.

Eldrack looked up and two huge knifebirds swooped down to him. He waved his wand and ropes wrapped around the birds' legs. He grabbed a rope with each hand and was picked up by the mighty creatures. He pulled on the ropes like parachute lines and steered the knifebirds to the moonstone. His sand beasts followed close behind him.

The tentacles of the sand beasts kicked up a cloud of sand and dust and showed their route over the dunes. The other knifebirds flew behind Eldrack in a huge "V" pattern. Now, there was nothing left but sand and heat to make their escape difficult. The only sound was the crackling of the fiery curtain around Derek, Tobungus, Zorell, and Dahlia. Deanna used the *Hydrolus* spell to put the fire out.

"Thanks, Deanna!" Derek called. Some of the water she had shot at them soaked his hair and cooled him down. The heat from the fire had made the desert seem so much hotter.

"No problem," Deanna replied, looking toward the dunes where Eldrack had flown. "We really need to get moving before Eldrack comes back."

"Deanna!" Derek yelled as she ran past, thinking about the moonstone.

"Not now," Deanna said. "We have to get out of here. Fast."

# 9 The Great Snort Pit

Derek and Deanna ran in front of the others for ten minutes before stopping to catch their breath. "Deanna," Derek managed to say between breaths, "we have to get the moonstone back."

Tobungus and Zorell looked at Deanna, hoping she had a plan. "No," she said, "we have to get back to Amemnop."

Derek began thinking about the prophecy. "Deanna, if Eldrack gets the power from the moonstone, his evil power will grow."

"Derek, we *really* need to get back to Amemnop," Deanna said.

"But why?" Derek asked.

At that moment, they heard a thunderous voice yell, "NO!" across the desert.

"That wasn't the moonstone I threw," Deanna laughed.

"What was it then?" Derek asked in amazement.

"I saw Eldrack's spells melting the sand," Deanna explained. "The molten blobs hardened into sand colored crystals. So, I used the wand to melt some sand into a fake moonstone."

"Brilliant!" Tobungus squealed.

"Yes, quite clever," Zorell added, "but I have to agree with Deanna. We really should get moving before Eldrack returns."

Behind them, they could see a cloud of dust swirling as the army of sand beasts charged toward them. They tried to run, but it was difficult. They struggled as their feet sank into the soft sand.

"This way," Dahlia called, pointing to a dune to their right. Everyone followed her as she struggled up the sandy hill.

When they reached the top, Dahlia said, "Over the next dune is the Great Snort Pit. We can find windriders on that dune and get far away from here."

"We've got to hurry," Tobungus said. "Eldrack is getting closer."

"I have an idea," Deanna said. She raised the wand and sent a jet of fire down the side of the dune to melt the sand. After about a minute or two, she changed from the fire spell to a blast of icy wind to freeze the molten sand. When she was done, a thick glass slide stretched down to the bottom of the dune.

"Cool!" cheered Derek and Dahlia together.

Derek dove head first, sliding down on his stomach. The others followed on their backs.

"That was great," Dahlia shouted. "I wish we could do it again."

As they ran up the next dune, they heard a series of loud snorts and grunts. Derek and Deanna looked at each other, but didn't take the time to stop and ask questions. When they reached the top of the dune, they saw a few of the windriders that Dahlia had mentioned.

The windriders looked like rowboats with hang gliders attached to them. Dahlia walked over to the nearest windrider and threw her pack aboard. Derek and Deanna couldn't help but notice that there were huge bite marks on the side of the windrider. Dahlia saw that Derek looked worried about the marks and said, "Yeah, we don't want to get the windrider too close to the mouth of the pit."

"The mouth?" Derek muttered.

"Don't worry," Dahlia said confidently. "I'll time it right. We just have to worry about flying too high."

"I wish that made me feel more comfortable," Derek said, looking uncertainly at the beat up windrider. But, he knew that it was their only hope. He simply shook his head and tossed his bag on top of Dahlia's.

"Come on," Dahlia said. "Help me push it to the edge."

The dune had a strange steep slope on the other side. Near the bottom, there was a wide hole with a cloud of sand swirling around it. A loud snort shot a blast of wind out, and the next snort sucked it back in.

"Everybody, get on," Dahlia said excitedly.

Derek, Deanna, and Zorell jumped on board, but Tobungus climbed in nervously. "If I can water ski, you can get on the windrider," Zorell teased.

"Deanna," Eldrack's voice boomed from the next dune, "you tricked me."

"Dahlia, whatever you're going to do, you better do it soon," Deanna said.

"Alright," Dahlia said, "as soon as the pit snorts out, we need to start down the dune."

They waited for several seconds and then heard a snort that sounded like a hundred hungry pigs. "Now!" Dahlia yelled. They leaned forward and the windrider started to slide down the sandy slope. Seconds later, another deafening snort began sucking the wind back in. The windrider was caught in the current and pulled toward the mouth of the pit.

After a few tense moments, the wind died down, and Dahlia pulled on the hang glider's rudder. The windrider raised up off of the dune's surface and began to fly over the snort pit.

"Now we have to make it to the other side of the mouth before the next snort," Dahlia said nervously. "Let's hope this thing is fast enough."

"What do you mean?" Tobungus asked.

"If we get caught over the pit," Dahlia said, concentrating on keeping the windrider flying in the direction they needed to go, "we will get shot straight up, and we'll probably lose control."

"This has been a really nice trip to the Desert Realm," Tobungus said sarcastically. "We'll have to be sure to come back really soon."

They held their breath as the windrider got to the center of the pit, and then continued on toward the other side. Dahlia exhaled as the next snort shot a blast of wind at the back of the windrider. The wind pushed them along and they rose into the sky. The windrider bobbed along gently just inside a thick layer of clouds.

Dahlia pulled a silver tube out of her bag. "I was hoping I would get to use this," she said. She held the tube out and waved it back and forth in the thick clouds. After a few seconds, she pulled it back and put it to her lips, like a straw. She took a long drink and said, "Cloud water is the most refreshing drink. It really hits the spot out here in the desert."

She showed the others how to use the cloud tapper, and they each took turns drinking the ice cold pure water. They sat back and enjoyed the gentle breezes and the way that the clouds seemed to dance along the edges of the boat.

When Eldrack finally reached the top of the dune overlooking the Great Snort Pit, he saw no sign of the children. The sand beasts looked at him nervously. He turned around and walked back down the dune without saying a word.

The windrider slowly came down near the edge of the Great Aquarian Divide on the wet sandy beach. When they reached the ground, Dahlia hopped out. "You guys can use the boat part of the windrider to get back to Amemnop," she said.

"That would be great," Derek said. "If we use the boat, we can avoid the ferryman."

"And this time, you won't have to tow me along," Zorell hissed.

"Aw, but that's so much fun," Tobungus said. Turning to Deanna, he added, "Can't you find a little scrap of driftwood or garbage to use as Zorell's skis?"

"It's been a long day, Tobungus," Deanna said, shaking her head and turning to Dahlia.

Dahlia shook their hands and said, "Thank you for stopping Eldrack and the sand beasts. Maybe we can get back to normal here."

"Dahlia, you helped a lot," Deanna said. "Everyone in Elestra would thank you if they knew what you did."

"Yeah," Derek said, "maybe someone will make a tapestry with your picture on it someday."

"That would be something to see," Dahlia said smiling. "I didn't think I would help you much today. I just wanted to come along to see you two."

"What do you mean?" Deanna asked.

"There are stories among my people about young wizards coming to free Roparcia from a wave of terrible creatures," Dahlia explained. "My grandmother has a tapestry that shows this legend. I've always loved that story."

Deanna had been thinking about something that bothered her. "Dahlia, we know Glabber who has used his powerful magic to protect Roparcia in the past. I can't figure out why he didn't come here to battle the sand beasts?"

"He is not the wizard who was foretold to battle the sand beasts," Dahlia explained.

Derek looked down at the scroll he was holding. "Does your grandmother's tapestry tell you what this scroll is?" he asked.

"Derek," Dahlia said nervously, "You have done so much for my people. I don't want to upset you, but I can't tell you anything. My grandmother always told me that I should not discuss the legends in the tapestries. I think the stories could change if people talked about them."

"Yes, I know that there are some strange rules about prophecies," Derek said.

Dahlia sighed and continued, "One time, late at night, I snuck into a hidden room in my grandmother's basement and saw another tapestry. I only got a quick look, but I think that it showed you and your sister." She paused for a moment. "It also showed that dark wizard we saw today."

"Did it show our battle with Eldrack in the Dunes?" Deanna asked.

"No, there was no battle," Dahlia began.

Derek cut her off. He was thinking about the prophecy that Gula Badu had shown him. "We probably shouldn't talk about this. If there's any chance that talking about it might change what happens, that could be bad. Let's just be happy that we got this moonstone and get on our way to Amemnop."

Dahlia looked relieved that Derek didn't press her for more information.

Deanna had one more question for Dahlia before they left. "Dahlia, how did your grandmother get the tapestries with the prophecies on them?"

"I know I didn't tell you this before," Dahlia said, "but my grandmother is the Queen of Roparcia."

Derek and Deanna stared at her in amazement. Dahlia continued, "My grandmother's really funny. She always liked to sneak around and get in trouble when she was a kid. She tells me that I remind her of herself. She and I have talked about the tapestries, but even she doesn't like it when I go to the house where we met this morning. She thinks it's too dangerous with the sand beasts lurking around."

Derek and Deanna stared at Dahlia, not knowing what to say. Dahlia laughed and reached into her pack. She handed a paper bag to Derek. "You'll need some extra lizard tails for your trip back to Amemnop."

After saying one last "goodbye," Derek reached in and grabbed one of the sweet treats. With bits of chewy lizard tail once again sticking to his teeth, he pushed away from shore, and they headed back toward the Magian side of the Divide.

# 10 The Unwritten Prophecy

The boat ride back to Amemnop took all night. Zorell told the others that he could see better in the dark, so he would stay up to steer them along. He was really hoping for a few hours of silence from Tobungus.

Derek and Deanna decided to look through the moonstone before getting back to Amemnop. After finding each moonstone, they had to look through it at the moon it was connected to. They always felt a warm rush of magical energy flow through their bodies as their magical powers increased.

Derek looked through the stone first. Once the wave of magic had washed over him, he handed the stone to Deanna. She raised the stone and looked at the moon through it.

"Whoa!" Derek said.

"What?" Deanna asked. She saw that his mouth was hanging open. "Derek, what's wrong?"

"Deanna," Derek said excitedly. When you looked through the stone, your eyes gave off green light. It was really bizarre."

Deanna looked at Zorell and Tobungus who nodded that they had seen it also. "Well, I don't know what happened," Deanna said. "I didn't feel any different. We'll have to ask Iszarre about it when we get back."

She and Derek talked for a few more minutes before falling into a dream-filled sleep. Tobungus spent the night snoring and talking in his sleep about sand and fleas. Every few minutes, Zorell smacked him with a rolled up scroll and told him that he was swatting flies away.

Just after the sun rose, the boat pulled up to a pier in Amemnop. Derek and Deanna stumbled off of the boat, still tired from their trip. Tobungus seemed wide awake, but Zorell said that he had to run off to get some sleep. He promised to meet them later that evening at Glabber's place.

Derek and Deanna finally made it to Glabber's and slowly walked to a table near the counter. "You look exhausted," Glabber called out.

"I don't think I've ever been this tired," Deanna said. "We had a long day in the desert."

"I have just the thing for you," Glabber said as he slithered into the kitchen. A few minutes later, he came back out with two glasses of blue liquid. "This is sleep juice," he said as he set the glasses on their table.

"But we don't want to go to sleep," Derek muttered.

"No, no," Glabber said quickly, "sleep juice does not make you sleep. It is liquid sleep. After you drink one glass, your body will feel refreshed and you will be able to stay awake all day."

"How does it work?" Deanna asked.

"There is a kind of bird called the Horned Slumber Hawk," Glabber explained. "The bird sleeps for weeks at a time in the psychic forest where oceanberry trees absorb the thoughts of people and animals who live there. It doesn't hurt the sleeping animals at all," he said in response to the twins' looks of alarm. "The oceanberry tree swallows the sleep energy of the Horned Slumber Hawks and uses it to form these wonderful blue berries. We take the berries and squeeze the juice out of them. When you drink the juice, you are actually drinking sleep."

Derek and Deanna drank the glasses of sweet blue juice and instantly felt awake and refreshed. "That's amazing," Derek blurted out.

"Yes, well, it's usually pretty expensive, but you two deserve some special treatment here," Glabber hissed before slithering back to the kitchen.

Derek pulled out the Lost Scroll of Roparcia and unrolled it gently. He stared at the thick, yellowed paper and sat motionless.

"What does it say?" Deanna asked excitedly.

"Nothing," Derek said, turning the scroll for her to see. The paper was empty.

"Ah, I see you have a story scroll," said Iszarre. The old wizard had come out of the kitchen to visit with them for a few minutes.

"Yeah, but it's blank," Derek said.

"Oh, no, Derek, it's not blank," Iszarre replied. "The story of your entire time in Elestra is there, but you don't know how to see it yet. A story scroll is used by people who have a strong connection to prophecies. It takes a special kind of magic to see into the flames of a prophecy. That same magic will flow from you onto this scroll."

"So it's just like a diary for our adventures," Derek replied somewhat disappointedly.

"No, no!" Iszarre said. "As you get stronger, you will find out that the parts of the story you put down will not end where you think they should. You will start to conjure up bits of information about your future adventures. You may never be able to see all of the details of your future journeys, but you will be able to get clues to help you along, and that will be a powerful weapon."

"But how do I do it?" Derek asked, looking at the blank scroll in a new light.

"Open the scroll and light a candle with a green flame," Iszarre explained. "When you look into the flame, you will not see a new prophecy, but you will tell the story to the scroll and the words will appear there."

"But how will I know what to say?" Derek asked, still unsure of himself.

Iszarre reached into one of the pockets of the robe that was squished under his apron and pulled out a candle. "This candle will help you get started."

Derek lit the candle and stared into the flickering fire. Tiny sparks looped across the scroll, and he could see the story of their trip down the bubbling river near Cauldron Lake and of the time they met Zorell in the Library. He looked up in amazement at Iszarre.

"Don't rush it, Derek," Iszarre said, blowing out the candle. "Let the story come out slowly. At night, when your day's adventures are done, look into the candle. As your power grows, the words will flow more easily. Before long, the story of the newest Mystical Guardians will have a home on this scroll."

"Oh, by the way," Deanna said, "I have something for you." She pulled out the necklace that the woman from the statue had given to her and handed it to the old wizard.

"My, my, my!" Iszarre said. "It looks like I have my work cut out for me today."

"What is that necklace?" Deanna asked.

"It is the key to the Dungeon of Oromar, the resting place of the Magical Army of Roparcia," Iszarre said. "With this key, I can make sure that the Roparcian Army is on our side." He looked at the amulet in the necklace, deep in thought. "Deanna, you may not know it, but you've been holding a piece of the Ruby Core today. Very few Elestrans have even seen a tiny chip from the Ruby." Finally, he stood up and said, "I must get going. I have a few stops to make before heading to Roparcia," he added mysteriously. "If you need anything while I am away, Glabber will be here to help."

He took one step away from the table and quickly spun back around. "I almost forgot," he said. "I think it's a good idea for you to take a few days off from looking for moonstones. You can explore Amemnop, see a concert, go to the zoo, eat something weird. That sort of thing."

"But we don't want to let Eldrack get a head start on the fourth moonstone," Derek replied.

"It's more important that you stay here for a while," Iszarre said. "You have just finished gathering the first set of three moonstones. Your power has grown by as much as a normal wizard's power grows in a whole year. If you move too quickly, you will not be able to absorb and retain the new powers that the moonstones will give to you. You have to give yourselves a few days of rest."

"Actually a few days in Amemnop without Eldrack around sounds pretty nice," Derek said.

"I guess that's not such a bad idea," Deanna added. "We've talked about going to the zoo, and I'm sure that there are some neat magic shops to explore."

"See, that's the spirit," Iszarre said. "Now, I'm off." He turned once again to leave.

"Wait," Deanna called. Iszarre looked back over his shoulder. "When I looked through the third moonstone, Derek said that my eyes gave off a green light. Do you know what that's all about?"

"Yes," Iszarre said, turning to leave again.

"Wait," Deanna blurted out again. "What does it mean?"

"Well, you just asked if I knew what it meant," Iszarre teased. Before Deanna could point out that he knew what she meant, he held up his hand and said, "It's a long story. Don't worry, though. It's another sign that your powers are growing rapidly. Listen, I really have to get going. How about I tell you all about it tomorrow morning over breakfast?"

Deanna nodded, and Iszarre hurried out of the diner.

Derek and Deanna were disappointed that Iszarre had left so quickly. Derek was hoping to learn more about the prophecies, and he knew that Iszarre had much more to say. He read through the words on his story scroll to see if there were any clues about their next adventure, but it only told about what they had already done.

After breakfast, they went for a walk through Amemnop, since they could not look through the moonstone and see the vision during the day. They had only seen a small part of the city and wanted to explore as much as possible now that they had the time. They reached a neighborhood with rows of small shops. As they walked along, a woman called out to Derek, "Young man, you look like you could use a haircut."

"Who me?" Derek said, pointing at himself.

"She's right, Derek," Deanna teased.

Derek had been thinking that he should get a haircut because his hair had been getting in his eyes as they ran through the sandy winds in the Desert Realm. "Alright," Derek said, to Deanna's surprise. "I'll get my hair cut."

He walked into the shop and sat in a normal looking barber's chair. "How do you want your hair cut?" the woman asked.

"Oh, I don't know," Derek replied. "Do whatever you normally do here in Amemnop. But not too short," he added.

"Very good," she said. She opened a fat ceramic jar and peered inside. "Hair fairies," she whispered, "wake up. We have a Magian boy cut to do."

A cloud of half-inch fairies flew out of the jar and circled his head. Within seconds, they were firing a barrage of magical spells at his hair. Each spell snipped another piece of hair. It felt like a thousand tiny hands were tickling his head. One of the hair fairies came close to his left ear and whispered, "How many pillars does Tarook have?"

"What?" Derek said turning his head quickly toward the voice. He was sure that the voice sounded like Iszarre, but all he saw was a swarm of buzzing hair fairies.

"Young man," the woman scolded, "you must keep still. You almost ended up with a shaved head."

"Sorry," Derek said, settling back into his chair.

Soon the haircut was complete and he joined Deanna back out in the street. He ran his hands through his hair, wondering how much the hair fairies had cut. "It looks fine," Deanna said. "It's still pretty long, but at least you can see now."

"Yeah, and if I don't like it, there's probably a spell to turn my hair purple or something," Derek said.

Deanna stopped and looked very frustrated. "I can't believe that we forgot to ask Iszarre where we're going next," she said. "How are we going to figure out where the next moonstone is hidden?"

"I have a feeling that we should look up the pillars of Tarook," Derek replied. Deanna looked questioningly at him. "Let's just say a little voice told me so."

They continued walking through Amemnop and had cheese cones and klom root soup for dinner outside a small restaurant. After dinner, the moons of Elestra began to rise, so they headed toward the Tower of the Moons.

They climbed the steep stairs to the top of the Tower. In the first moments of darkness on a warm Magian evening, Deanna placed the third Moonstone into the Arch. After finding each moonstone, they came to the Tower and put the stone in the arch on the top floor. Iszarre had performed a powerful spell on the arch which would protect the stones from Eldrack.

The first set of three stones was in place. Iszarre had told them that each set of three moonstones unlocked a magical instrument. When all five instruments had been unlocked, their combined song would call the Lost Army of Light. The sound of a harp playing haunting music was faint in the air. It seemed to be struggling to escape from the moonstones.

The song was just starting, but they knew that somewhere, an army of magical warriors could barely hear the musical notes that would become their anthem.

Deanna closed her eyes and listened to the soft sounds. "That must be the music of the first magical instrument."

"It's not very loud, though," Derek replied. "It's going to have to be louder than that to call the Lost Army of Light."

"Maybe when all of the instruments play together, the music gets louder," Deanna said. She looked at the rest of the arch stretching out over their heads. Their quest was starting to seem possible, and yet, there were still twelve open slots on the arch.

# The Third Vision

"It's time to look through the moonstone to see the next vision," Deanna said. Derek moved close to Deanna, and they both looked through the third moonstone at the yellow moon overhead.

Instantly, they felt the heat of Roparcia. A man in a long purple robe stood in the same room in the pyramid where they had been the day before. They realized that the man was Gelladrell, the third Mystical Guardian. He was talking to a woman. He seemed to be in a hurry. They kept turning their heads as if they heard sounds that weren't there. They seemed to sense that there was danger outside.

Gelladrell turned and ran through the opening into the passageway that led out of the pyramid. Moments later, Eldrack walked into the room with his wand in his hand. For the first time, they could hear what the people in the vision were saying. Eldrack walked right up to the woman and said, "Where is the moonstone?"

"The Labyrinth is a difficult challenge," the woman said bravely.

"I didn't ask about the Labyrinth," Eldrack shot back. "I asked about the moonstone." He waited a moment. "Oh, I see. You're saying that Gelladrell hid the moonstone in the Labyrinth."

"Evil and clever," the woman said. "You'll never find the moonstone, but why don't you go into the Labyrinth and spend a couple of centuries looking for it?"

"Very funny," Eldrack said. "I bet you think that I don't know how to enter the Labyrinth." He saw that her expression changed. "Yes, that's right. I know about the arches. I just sent the Labyrinth some new residents."

"What do you mean?" the woman asked.

"Those pesky purple dragons that your sisters sent to protect Gelladrell," Eldrack hissed. "They got too close to one of the arches, and a mighty wind carried them through to the Labyrinth. That's too bad. Now, who will protect the Dragon King?" His orange eyes seemed to flash with anger.

"No!" the woman said. "You must be stopped!" She reached for her wand.

"Perhaps, but not by you," Eldrack said, raising his wand. "*Edify*!" he shouted. A spray of white dust swirled around the woman who turned into a stone statue. "You can stay like this until the moonstone is found," Eldrack said quietly.

Eldrack walked up to the statue and stood silently. It looked like he was checking to make sure that the woman really was frozen in stone. Then, he turned and left the room.

The vision faded. Derek and Deanna stood up and stretched. "So, Eldrack turned her into a statue, and she was freed because we found the moonstone," Deanna said.

"Looks that way," Derek replied. "We should look through the other moonstones now." He saw that Deanna looked confused. "Iszarre told us that when we had a set of three, our ability to see the visions would increase, and that we could go back and look through the other stones to see more details. It sure seems like our power has increased. We heard Eldrack and that woman speak this time."

"You're right," Deanna said. "Let's start with the first moonstone." They turned to the first moonstone that they had found and lined up so that they could see the first moon through it.

The vision started quickly. They saw the moment when the moonstone had been picked up by the huge bird and then dropped into the dark Amemnop night. Eldrack turned to attack Baladorn, the first of the Mystical Guardians from their family. The first time they had attempted to view the vision, he had dissolved into a cloud and floated away from the Tower.

The scene shifted to a farmhouse. Baladorn was sitting at a rough wooden table, drinking from a heavy mug. He was alone, but it seemed as if someone had just left. "Unbelievable," Baladorn muttered to himself. He seemed to be trying to calm down after his battle with Eldrack. After several minutes, he stood up and looked around. "Are you coming back?" he called out a window.

There was no response. "How long does it take to get eggs?" he whispered to himself. He looked around the rustic room and saw an unusual carving that looked like a hand carved from dark wood sitting above the fireplace. He looked closely at it, as if he were thinking about what he was seeing. There was a click behind him. When he turned, Eldrack was standing in the doorway.

"Don't even try to go for your wand," Eldrack said.

"What have you done with him?" Baladorn asked worriedly.

"I just made it harder to find the eggs," Eldrack said. "I only need a moment to take you to your new home." Before Baladorn could respond, Eldrack said, "*Slumbero.*" Baladorn feel into a deep sleep. As the vision faded, Eldrack walked toward Baladorn.

"Well, I guess we just saw the moment when Baladorn was captured," Deanna said.

Derek nodded. "It really helps to hear what they're saying. We better look through the second stone before the moon is out of range."

They moved to their left and lined up the second moonstone. They were taken to the moment when Eldrack fired the massive wave of magical energy at the walls that Mindoro, the second Mystical Guardian, had built around himself. The scene was in the Atteelian Orchard where Derek and Deanna had found the second moonstone. As Eldrack climbed up the pile of rubble to search for Mindoro, everything slowed down. They could see the details of what was happening much more clearly.

Eldrack reached the top of the pile and looked toward the planting sheds. The first time they had seen the vision, they thought that he vanished from the pile, but this time, something was different. Instead of vanishing, he seemed to be sucked into the ground, exactly where Mindoro had been standing.

The vision ended there. The twins blinked and looked at each other in surprise. "That was quick," Derek said.

Deanna nodded. "I expected a lot more. We did learn one thing, though. Something pulled Eldrack down into the ground. He didn't just vanish."

"That's true," Derek said. "We also saw him looking around. It's lucky that he didn't go to search the planting sheds."

"That's for sure," Deanna said. She looked at the rest of the arch again. "We still have a long way to go, Derek."

Derek didn't say anything. He seemed unusually quiet. She suddenly realized that something had been bothering him since they had left the library on their way to Roparcia. "What's wrong, Derek?" she asked softly.

Derek reached into his pocket and slowly pulled out a folded piece of parchment paper. He handed it to her, and before she could ask what it was, he said, "This is about you too."

"I don't understand," Deanna said.

"Just read it," Derek replied. He walked over to a bench on the far side of the room and sat down, deep in thought.

Deanna opened the crinkly paper and read the words that Derek had seen in the Archive of Prophecies:

> *The Realms of Elestra will be torn asunder as the Five Hundred Year Battle nears. A rising tide of evil will imperil the land and endanger the rightful ruler. Through the mists of magical battle, two powerful wizards will emerge. They will complete many quests and fight many battles in the name of their King. They will take their places among Elestra's most powerful wizards, but they will struggle with a fateful decision. Following a terrible act of betrayal, the young wizards, first the sister, then the brother, will join their sworn enemy in the final battle.*

Her look darkened and she read the prophecy again. "It's not possible," she whispered to herself. She looked back at the arch and then walked out onto the balcony high above Amemnop. The wind blew through her flowing brown hair. The moons above shone down like protective guardians.

As she stared out over the City of Light, she sensed something stirring in the magic that flowed through this great land. She took in a deep breath and said, "Wherever you are, Eldrack, I will never join you."

In a dark room, far from Amemnop, a hooded figure sat at a table with only a single candle and a crystal ball. Within the mists of the crystal ball, Deanna appeared on the balcony of the Tower of the Moons. The figure pulled back his hood, to reveal a long scar down his left cheek. Without taking his glowing orange eyes off of the image, he whispered, "Yes, Deanna, you will join me. The second prophecy is coming true."

Turn the page. The adventure continues...

# Epilogue

Derek and Deanna have now found the first three moonstones and defeated Eldrack and his minions in Amemnop, the Atteelian Orchard, and the Desert Realm, but there is much more to do and much more to learn.

In their bits of free time, Deanna and Derek continue to wander through the State Library of Magia and other places in Amemnop to find out more about the places, people, and creatures they have encountered. The following pages will tell you what they learned, and perhaps, more importantly, what they didn't learn.

# A Day Off

Derek and Deanna spent the day after their return from the Desert Realm walking through Amemnop, enjoying the cool breeze. It was a day to relax, so they avoided going to the library or discussing the prophecy that Derek had read in the Archive with Gula Badu.

They visited a magic shop that specialized in citrus fruits. They found lemon perfume that acted as a spray-on shield and ground orange peel packets which could be added to magical soups to increase their power.

They both realized that Tobungus would love this shop and vowed to bring him the next time they shopped there. Deanna settled on the lemon perfume and three lemons so that she could have her own stash of the magical fruit.

Derek was surprised to find that the shop had a huge candle section. While he looked at the magical candles, he listened to the shopkeeper tell him all about the different colors of flames.

He was looking for candles with green flames, but he heard about blue-flamed healing candles, purple-flamed defensive candles, and the rare black-flamed candles used by the seers who looked into the future to write the prophecies in the many archives scattered across Elestra.

He ended up buying a pack of green-flamed candles, so the shopkeeper threw in a blue-flamed candle for free.

Their next stop was a clothing store that sold clothes from all of Elestra's realms. They had all the clothes they needed back in their room at Glabber's place, but they thought it would be fun to get some Elestran clothes to blend in more.

After picking out several pairs of loose-fitting pants and shirts that came down to their knees, which was a fashion among kids in Amemnop, Deanna asked about getting a wizard's robe. The shop went silent. All of the shoppers knew who Derek and Deanna were, and they were waiting to see what the tailor would say.

The tailor who owned the shop was an impossibly old man. His movements made him look like he needed to have his joints oiled. He told Deanna and Derek that all wizards have to be specially fitted for robes. They thought that this meant that he would have to measure them.

Instead, the old tailor pointed to a mirror on the far wall and said, "Point your wand at that mirror and say the words on this piece of paper." He handed Deanna a tattered scrap of paper and stepped back to watch her.

Deanna looked at the paper and raised the wand. "*Magicum Obviosa*!" she said loudly. A thick jet of green light shot from the wand and bounced off of the mirror. The shop was filled with tiny beams of green light that shot between the mirror and rows of jewels and beads lining the walls.

"Very well," the old man said. "And, now for you, young man." He nodded toward Derek.

Derek stepped to the spot where Deanna had been. She handed him the wand and said, "Be confident, Derek."

Derek took a deep breath and raised the wand. "*Magicum Obviosa*!" he said in a voice that almost sounded angry. A bolt of purple light shot from the wand with a blinding flash.

"One week," the old man said. "Your robes will be ready to pick up then."

Deanna noticed that the other shoppers were staring at them with their mouths hanging open. She and Derek gathered their bags and hurried out of the shop, thinking that a meal by the River of Tranquility would be a good idea.

As they sat, eating something utterly indescribable from the Torallian Forest, Tobungus' home, Derek said, "So, do you think we will ever get used to trying out magical spells and having crowds of people stare at us as if we had left the house in our underwear?"

Deanna laughed, but instead of answering, she took another bite of food. "I guess you have to be Torallian to appreciate the flavor."

Derek nodded and asked, "What should we look up when we go to the library tomorrow?"

"Good question," Deanna replied. "I was thinking that we might want to learn a little bit more about our aunts. Meeting the statue in the pyramid makes me think that they may be important in the stories of some of the moonstones."

"That sounds like a great place to start," Derek said, turning back to the bizarre food that was changing its color and shape to match his fingers. He had already bitten one of his own fingers by mistake, so he had to be careful.

# Sisterhood of the Ruby Dawn

The next morning, Derek and Deanna headed straight to the library to start their research on their mother's family. Even though they had been to the library several times, the sight of the towering shelves and thousands of candles always took their breath away.

Deanna walked to the fairy librarian's desk and asked for books on the Sisterhood of the Ruby Dawn. As soon as the librarian repeated their request, a wave of sparks guided her gaze to a row of books whose titles were brightly lit. The book fairies swooped out and gathered the books to take to the table where Derek had set their packs.

Deanna pulled the wand out and said, "*Explanatum,*" while touching the cover of the book on top of the stack. "Please tell me about the Sisterhood of the Ruby Dawn."

The top book hopped off of the pile and spun around twice, almost as if it was dancing. It settled onto the table and opened its cover and flipped to page 87. "Ooh, the Sisterhood of the Ruby Dawn," the book whispered. The book seemed to take a breath, and then a voice that struggled to hide its excitement said:

*The Sisterhood of the Ruby Dawn is a secretive group of women who guard many of Elestra's most important magical sites. The group's members are rarely seen, but most people sense that they are around.*

*Members of the Sisterhood are all sisters from the same family. There have been twenty-four sets of twins in this family, with forty-seven of the children being girls. All of the female children are members of the Sisterhood. The one brother is not associated with this group.*

*The Sisterhood began their work as guardians of the magical wells spread throughout Elestra, but they have branched out to other types of magical sites. They have been reported in all of the Six Kingdoms.*

"I hope that was helpful," the book said eagerly.

"Oh, yes," Deanna said, "Thank you." After the book had scooted off to the corner of the table, she turned to the next book and said, "Are the women in the Sisterhood wizards like Iszarre?"

The book groaned as it dragged its tired cover open. After a series of sighs, the book said:

> *The Sisterhood of the Ruby Dawn is made up of magical channelers who use magic differently than wizards such as the Paramage Iszarre. The Sisters are able to absorb magic directly from the Magic Wells.*
>
> *The Sisters usually work in pairs and share the magic that they absorb. If there are more than two of them present, they can magnify their power. Any of the Sisters can work together, but they will have the strongest bond with their twin.*
>
> *The Sisters can collect magic at many other places in Elestra, including fountains, magical streams, and forests where magic-collecting trees grow.*

*Magic channelers are wizards who use waves of magic, instead of magic spells. They study magic from an early age and can shape the waves so that they can do the same things as regular spells.*

*The advantage of magic waves is that multiple channelers can work together to make the magic flow from different starting points. Four channelers surrounding an enemy can combine their power to make waves of magic hit the target from all sides, making it very hard to create a successful defense.*

The book closed its cover and slunk to the corner with the first book.

Deanna turned to Derek and gave him a look that said that he should come up with the next question. He looked at the stack of books and said, "Do you have any information on a member of the Sisterhood of the Ruby Dawn named Ariel?"

The bottom book struggled to get out from under a thick, heavy book that rested on top of it. It was winded, but it threw its cover open and said:

*Ariel is the name of one of the Sisters of the Sisterhood of the Ruby Dawn. She is the one sister whose twin is not a female. Her twin is a brother who is not part of the Sisterhood.*

*Ariel is married to a Mystical Guardian and has a set of twin children who do not live in Elestra.*

*Even though Ariel is a powerful channeler, she has acted as an organizer for the Sisterhood. Since she does not have a twin who works with her, she guides her Sisters on their choice of sites to protect.*

*Most observers believe that Ariel is so powerful because she got all of the magic abilities that are usually divided among twins. This would explain her brother's refusal to join the Sisterhood's work.*

*Others think that both Ariel and her brother are very powerful, but that her brother did not want to be the one brother in a sisterhood.*

The book stopped talking, but it kept its cover open, indicating that it had more information on the Sisterhood.

Deanna had been thinking about what they had heard and said, "Why did the Sisterhood choose the name *Ruby Dawn*?"

The book continued:

*There is confusion over the name of the Sisterhood. Most people thought that the name Ruby Dawn referred to the Magical Wells which are the source of magic coming to the surface from the Ruby Core.*

*Since all magic in Elestra flows out of the Magical Wells, it is possible think of those locations as the dawn where magic starts. Since the Sisterhood started out as a group protecting the Wells, this seemed to make sense, but none of the Sisters would ever confirm this explanation, and some even suggested that it was wrong.*

*None other than the great wizard Iszarre hinted at a different meaning behind the name, when he said that after the long night, the Sisterhood would protect the Ruby Dawn. In his typical style, Iszarre never explained these words.*

The book went silent. Derek and Deanna looked at each other to see if there were any other questions to ask about the Sisterhood, but neither thought of any.

"Thank you," Deanna said. The book closed its cover and joined the others that had finished telling them about the Sisterhood.

"Wait a second," Derek said. "Do any of you books know about members of the Sisterhood helping the Mystical Guardian named Gelladrell in the Desert Realm?"

The book that had just finished rushed back and opened its cover. It said:

> *The Sisterhood of the Ruby Dawn has assisted the Mystical Guardians in their work when asked to do so. There was a rumor that Deleece, one of the Sisters, went to Roparcia at the urgent request of Gelladrell. Both Deleece and Gelladrell disappeared, but no details about that are available.*
>
> *Also, the Sisterhood worked closely with the Roparcian Royal Family to investigate the disappearances, but no information was found.*

*Members of the Sisterhood have visited the Desert Realm many times to maintain the safety of the Realm's Well.*

*The Sisterhood always has a member at the Roparcian Academy of Magic inside the Glass Mountain. The Sisters rotate at the Academy, so that none of them have to be away from the Wells for too long.*

The book stopped and slowly eased back to the corner, wondering if their questions were done.

"I guess that does it for the Sisterhood," Derek said. "I can't believe that our own mother is a member of the Sisterhood, and we never knew it."

"Yeah, well, we never knew that Dad was a Mystical Guardian, either," Deanna said.

"True," Derek replied. "Okay, so we learned that the Sisters use magic in a different way and that we may run into them if we go to magical places in Elestra. I can't think of anything else to ask about them now. Can you?"

"No, I think we're done with the Sisterhood, for now," Deanna said. "But, it was interesting that the book mentioned the Roparcian Royal Family. It made me think of the prophecy that Dahlia told us about. The one on the tapestry hidden in her grandmother's house."

"I wish we could talk to Dahlia again," Derek said. "But the books are the next best thing." He got up and walked over to the librarian's desk to request their next set of books.

# Roparcian Royalty

"Did you find what you needed about the Sisterhood of the Ruby Dawn?" the fairy librarian asked.

"I think so," Derek replied. "Who knows, we may be back to find out more about them later. But for now, we'd like to see books about the Roparcian Royal Family."

"Is that the current royal family?" the librarian asked.

"Yes, I guess so," Derek answered.

The librarian repeated his request, and two books lit up on the bottom shelf of the nearest wall. Derek was thinking that he could just grab the books, but the book fairies beat him to the shelves and whisked the books to the table where Deanna was sitting.

Deanna waved the wand toward the books and said, *"Explanatum."* She followed that by saying, "Please tell us about the Roparcian Royal Family.

Both books stood up, but neither opened their cover or said anything. The larger book finally opened its cover slightly and said, "Please go first," to the other book.

The second book immediately said, "No, I insist, you are the wiser book."

The two books went on like this for several minutes before Derek finally moved one of the books in front of him and said, "Okay, I don't really care which of you has the best manners. What I want to know is what you can tell me about the Roparcian Royal Family."

The first book said, "Well, if you insist," and opened its cover. It settled on page 16 and said:

> *Roparcia is ruled by Queen Creeobba, of the Pentarkh Family which has ruled Roparcia for over four centuries. The Pentarkhs have earned a reputation as fun-loving rulers.*
>
> *According to Roparcian laws written by the Pentarkhs, each town is required to have three circuses, eight parades, and thirty carnivals each year. They also require free juggling classes for all Roparcian citizens.*

*Roparcians have always loved the rulers from the Pentarkh family because they make life in the desert so much fun.*

The book went silent, so Deanna asked, "Can you tell us more about Queen Creeobba?"

*Queen Creeobba has ruled Roparcia for sixty-seven years. She married a prince from Drellacia on the far side of the Desert Realm, and they have seven children.*

*Under Roparcian law, once a person reaches forty years of age, they cannot become king or queen. Six of Creeobba's children are already past the age of disqualification. If Creeobba continues to rule for just one more year, all of her children will be ineligible to rule Roparcia.*

*The title of ruler would then skip a generation and go to one of Creeobba's grandchildren. The rules for determining which grandchild would take the throne are complicated and may not be fully known until the choice is to be made.*

The book started to close its cover, but added, "Now, I really must insist that you allow the other book a chance to answer some of your questions. It's only fair."

Deanna laughed and turned to the second book. "Please tell me whether you have any information about the Roparcian Royal Family and the Sisterhood of the Ruby Dawn working together," Deanna said.

The second book was more than happy to plop down in front of Deanna and whip its cover open. A proud voice said:

> *I most certainly can tell you about this exciting partnership. Let's see, where to start.*
>
> *The Sisterhood of the Ruby Dawn is known throughout Elestra, and when the Roparcian king called, they were happy to help. It seems as if one of the Mystical Guardians had business in Roparcia and ran into some kind of trouble.*
>
> *Now, between you and me, I don't see how a Mystical Guardian could get in trouble, but I just repeat what is written on my pages.*

*Anyhoo, when the Mystical Guardian needed help, the King of Roparcia summoned the Sisterhood. They immediately sent Deleece, one of their strongest members.*

*Okay, now this is where it gets positively outrageous. Not only did the Mystical Guardian disappear, but Deleece was never seen again either. Can you believe that?*

*Now, most kings would have lost their throne over such a scandalous situation. I mean, losing a Mystical Guardian and one of the Sisters. Come on!*

*So, where was I? Oh, yes. The King called the Sisterhood to his castle and went with them to investigate, but no one could find any evidence to explain what had happened.*

*Then, get this. The King had a party in honor of Deleece and Gelladrell. That was the name of the lost Mystical Guardian. A party!*

*Now, this is what is so typically Roparcian. They decided to keep having the party every year. Now it is a huge Roparcian Festival that spans five days and brings visitors from all parts of Elestra.*

*I just love the Roparcians. Don't you?*

The book closed its cover and gasped for breath after its quick, excited discussion about Roparcia.

Derek and Deanna looked at each other and laughed. This book was not like the others. It was more like a friend who talked to them, than a teacher who lectured them.

"Thank you so much," Deanna said. She waved to the book fairies who flew in and took the books back to their shelf.

"What's next?" Derek asked.

"Food!" Deanna replied. "We haven't eaten in hours."

"Okay, just promise me that we won't get anything from the Torallian Forest again," Derek said. "My fingers still hurt." He shook his hand to emphasize the pain from biting his own fingers instead of the camouflaged food.

"Well, then, why don't we try to find a Roparcian restaurant," Deanna suggested. "After hearing about Roparcia and Dahlia's family, I think it would be kind of neat to see the types of food that they eat."

"You mean besides lizard tails?" Derek asked playfully.

"Yeah, like what sorts of meals do they eat," Deanna said. "Although, a lizard tail for dessert wouldn't be bad."

"The perfect dessert from the desert," Derek said.

They walked out through the giant library doors and let their eyes adjust to the bright sun. They headed toward the river and a street where you could find just about any type of restaurant.

They were enjoying their three days of rest, but they knew that before long, they would have to find out exactly who Tarook was and why he had pillars.

# Preview of Book 4

Derek and Deanna seek the fourth moonstone in *The Seven Pillars of Tarook.* With the first set of moonstones in the arch, the twins start their search for the second set on the bitterly cold side of Mt. Drasius. There they meet a band of kangaroos who specialize in snowball fights.

Before they even get to Mt. Drasius, Zorell has a run-in with a jellybird, and Deanna has some explaining to do to a group of rocks.

Zorell loved the Desert Realm, and he would love the hot side of Mt. Drasius where many of his species live, but he is not accustomed to the icy conditions that they face when they finally locate the architect Tarook's greatest creation.

As Deanna and Derek have come to expect, Eldrack is out to get the moonstone and tries to stop the twins once again. Their harrowing battle under an icy temple held up by thin pillars will be decided by . . . *used socks*?

The first chapter of the twins' fourth adventure in Elestra begins on the next page, and the story ends in the pages of *The Seven Pillars of Tarook.*

# 1 Pancakes and Prophecies

Deanna Hughes woke up early. At least, she thought it was early. "Derek," she mumbled, wondering whether her twin brother was still sleeping.

"Yeah, Deanna," Derek said from across the room. "The sun just came up about ten minutes ago. I didn't expect you to wake up for an hour or two."

"Why are you up?" she asked, still shaking the web of sleep from her mind.

"I've been getting up early lately," he answered.

"Are you alright?" She was worried that he was getting depressed about being away from their parents.

They had been transported to the magical world of Elestra where they were racing to find the powerful moonstones before the dark wizard Eldrack could get his hands on them. They had made new friends, including Tobungus, the mushroom man, and Zorell, a talking cat. These two seemed to hate each other, which often led to entertaining arguments.

They also spent time with two powerful wizards, Iszarre and Glabber. Iszarre was a human wizard who also worked as a cook at Glabber's restaurant. They had found out that Iszarre was an award-winning chef, and that the snake Glabber was a leading wizard from the Desert Realm.

Over the past three days, Derek and Deanna had explored Amemnop, the capital of Magia, one of the Kingdoms of Elestra. They went to museums, magic shops, and bakeries. They bought Elestran clothes and ate lots of new foods, some good and some not so good. At one shop, Deanna bought lemon perfume, and Derek bought a collection of green-flamed candles for his story scroll.

The most unusual place they visited was the Magian Zoo and Bestiary where bizarre creatures from all over Elestra were paid to live and tell visitors about themselves. After looking at the directory of creatures at the zoo, Derek and Deanna sat down for a nice long talk with a knifebird.

Eldrack had used knifebirds to attack them in the Desert Realm, where they found the third moonstone. They wanted to know why the knifebirds followed Eldrack. Their earlier research on Eldrack's minions revealed that some of the groups following Eldrack had been angry at King Barado because of disagreements over music.

The knifebird told them that a flock of knifebirds had flown to the Antikrom Mountains to sell extra feathers and had never returned. This flock showed up at Eldrack's side a year later.

The bird also explained that knifebird feathers could be used to absorb magical liquids, such as healing potions or sleep juice, to be used later. When he learned that Derek and Deanna were Mystical Guardians, the knifebird gave them each a feather for their adventures yet to come.

As usual, the twins had left the interview with just as many questions as they had answers. They knew that only time would reveal the significance of what the knifebird had told them.

Deanna thought back on all they had done, but she realized that sometimes even all of Elestra's uniqueness was not enough to stop them from being homesick.

"Oh, yeah, I'm fine," Derek said, sensing that Deanna thought he was getting homesick. "Being here alone is getting easier, actually." He walked to the window and continued. "I just can't get the prophecy out of my mind. Can it be true that we'll join Eldrack?"

"No way!" Deanna nearly yelled. "Absolutely not!"

"Well, the prophecy seemed pretty sure," Derek said, still looking out the window.

"I'm telling you, Derek, we won't ever join Eldrack." She was suddenly wide awake. "We've seen what he's done. He has so many generations of our family in those awful tubes in the Cave of Imprisonment, and he's after us."

"Is he really, Deanna?" Derek asked. Before she could reply, he continued, "He's powerful. There's no doubt about that. He knows Elestra better than we do. He's had his chances if he wanted to capture us. Why hasn't he?"

"Maybe he needs us to get the moonstones," she said. "He's always trying to steal them from us."

"But why do we need to get the moonstones instead of him?" Derek asked. "He possesses enough magic to do the things we've done."

"I'll agree that he is strong," Deanna said. "Hmm. Maybe each Mystical Guardian put a protective spell on the moonstones when they were hidden so that they could only be found by other Mystical Guardians."

"Well, Iszarre never said anything about that," Derek said. "But, there's a lot that Iszarre hasn't said. It's like he wants us to figure things out on our own."

"We've learned that some magic is affected by talking about it," Deanna said. "It's like those prophecies where you're not supposed to talk about them. Remember how Dahlia didn't want to talk about the prophecy in her grandmother's house? That was about us, and she knew that if she talked about it, everything could change."

Derek nodded as Deanna spoke. She continued, "Maybe Iszarre can't tell us about the Mystical Guardians' spells because telling us would break the spells."

Derek was thinking about the moonstones they had found. He finally said, "It's possible that the Mystical Guardians put protective spells on the moonstones, but Tobungus was the one who found the stone in the Atteelian Orchard."

"But I was the one who popped the stone out of the stain-glass window," Deanna interrupted.

"So, it's possible," Derek said. "But, I'm still not sure."

"Okay, maybe Eldrack's trying to trick us," Deanna suggested. "Maybe he wants us to stop fearing him, or even to trust him. Then, when he makes his move for the moonstones, he can try to get our help. Does that sound possible?"

"Yeah, I was actually thinking that," Derek replied. "You know, that he thinks he can trick us."

Deanna could see that there was still concern in Derek's eyes. "We'll just have to be careful, Derek."

"I think we're missing something, Deanna," Derek said quietly.

"All that I'm missing right now is breakfast," Deanna said, trying to lighten the mood.

"Well, I'm sure that Glabber will have something interesting for us this morning," Derek said, allowing Deanna to change the subject. He realized that they weren't going to figure out Eldrack's strategies yet, and he was hungry.

Deanna got dressed and gathered the wand and a few other things to put in her backpack. After making sure that they hadn't forgotten anything, they walked down to the diner below. Glabber's Grub Hut was busy, even at such an early hour, but that didn't stop the great serpent chef from slithering over to their table as soon as they sat down. Glabber took a long look at the children and hissed, "A special breakfast will do you some good."

"What do you mean?" Derek asked.

"Young man," Glabber said, "I have seen the dark clouds of fear, worry, and anger shroud the faces of enough people to know that you are consumed by thoughts of something mysterious."

"He's alright, Glabber," Deanna said, "It's just that he can't stop thinking about a prophecy that suggested that something bad will happen at the end of our quest."

"Prophecies are like looking into a rippling lake," Glabber said, trying to reassure them. "You see a reflection on the surface, but you don't know exactly what you are seeing. The words may be obscured by the ripples of the meaning that you think you read."

"I don't know. This prophecy seemed pretty clear," Derek replied.

"All prophecies do," Glabber hissed. "There is much more for you to learn before you can even try to understand the meaning of a prophecy such as this." He began to slither back to the kitchen. "I will get your breakfast. Food can be a great ally when you are trying to solve a puzzle. I have just the thing to help you clear your mind, so that you can focus on this pesky prophecy."

A moment later, the great wizard Iszarre, wearing a flowing purple robe under his grimy apron, dropped into a chair across from Deanna. "What's this I hear about a prophecy?" he asked.

Deanna wanted to keep the actual prophecy secret, so she said, "Derek's just a little bit worried about a prophecy he read. It might have suggested that we would not succeed in our quest."

"My dear Deanna," Iszarre said with a mix of anger and laughter, "let me tell you something about prophecies." He stroked his chin. "Many, many years ago, I read the words of a prophecy in a candle's flame. It foretold of an epic struggle that I would face. It said that my wand, my greatest weapon, would be unable to help me."

Deanna leaned forward. "What happened?" she asked, dying to know what happened.

"I prepared for months," Iszarre said seriously. "I practiced every defensive spell I knew, and I even tried to make up some new ones. Then one day, I was in the kitchen at a restaurant where I was working, when three men in dark robes walked in through the front door."

He could see that Derek's and Deanna's attention was fixed on him. "I had thirty pancakes on the griddle, and I had just set my wand in the jar with all of my other kitchen tools. In my haste to grab my wand, I knocked a jar of Blastolian sugarbush nectar over. The nectar is the stickiest substance in Elestra. It oozed into the jar of utensils. My wand was stuck. So were the pancake turners."

"Is that when the dark wizards came into the kitchen?" Deanna asked.

"You see, Deanna," Iszarre said, "You have fallen for the trap of any prophecy. You expected a battle with dark wizards. To be fair, that is what I expected. Those men were simply hungry Fradoolian crab traders, however. The real battle was with the thirty pancakes that were starting to burn on the griddle. I couldn't get my wand. But more importantly, I couldn't get a pancake turner. What could I do?"

He thought for a moment and laughed. "The other chef in the kitchen was very young," he said. "He smelled the burning pancakes and ran over to help. On the way, he tripped over a pot, knocked at least a hundred glasses to the floor, and let out a string of spells from his wand as he landed in a puddle of grease. It took hours to undo his spells."

"Okay, so that was a goofy prophecy," Derek said. "Our prophecy is much more serious."

"Derek, you don't understand how important my prophecy was," Iszarre replied.

"I don't mean to be rude, but I don't think that a battle with thirty burning pancakes can compare to joining Eldrack," Derek said, and then realized that he let the terrible part of the prophecy slip out.

To his and Deanna's surprise, Iszarre didn't even react to the idea that they would join Eldrack. "Don't you see, Derek, I read my prophecy and assumed something truly terrible would happen. I focused all of my attention on what I thought would happen. I wasn't ready to use simple magic in a situation that might happen every day. I learned on that day that I should never let a prophecy dominate my vision. I also learned that the words of a prophecy can have many meanings."

Deanna had been thinking through the words of the prophecy. She couldn't remember all of them, but she had most memorized after reading it over and over.

"Iszarre," she said, "I've been thinking about what the prophecy said, and I don't think that it could have a different meaning than we are thinking."

Iszarre nodded and a slight smile crossed his face. "Deanna, did the prophecy use Eldrack's name?" he asked in a quiet voice.

"No, but it said the dark wizard," Deanna replied.

"Actually it said 'their sworn enemy' I think," Derek corrected.

"Oh, yeah, that's right," Deanna said.

"Well, you already have many friends," Iszarre said. "It is possible that you will gather more enemies along the way as well. You have twelve more moonstones to find. While you are doing that, you will have plenty of time to ponder the meaning of 'sworn enemy.'"

Derek was about to say something, but Iszarre said, "Ah, I see Glabber's coming with a platter of dancing Yahoran melons, spicy waffles, and ice cold Vidolan goat milk. Delicious!"

# Peekaboo Pepper Books

The line-up of Peekaboo Pepper Books is expanding quickly. We would like to take this opportunity to provide short previews of other upcoming titles in the *Guardians of Elestra* series.

*The Dark City: Guardians of Elestra #1*

Deanna and Derek follow their grandfather to Elestra where they learn that they are the last hope against a dark wizard in a race to collect the magical moonstones. They'll need all the help they can get from Tobungus, the tap-dancing mushroom man, Iszarre, the powerful wizard/fry cook, and Glabber, the snake wizard. Talking books, book fairies, flying coyote birdmen, devious hot peppers, and a short-tempered frog make their first adventure in Elestra one to remember.

*The Giants of the Baroka Valley: Guardians of Elestra #2*

Deanna and Derek set out on their second adventure in Elestra with Tobungus the mushroom man at their side. Along the way, they meet Zorell, a cat who has a hate/hate relationship with Tobungus, and ride a giant goose to the Baroka Valley. In the land where everything is huge, from the plants and animals to the grains of sand on a beach, they face off against Eldrack, fend off some sickening gong music, and sail down the River of the Dragon's Breath on an unusual boat. In the end, they are left with a new mystery and a plate of panpies (er, pancakes).

*The Seven Pillars of Tarook: Guardians of Elestra #4*
(available July 2011)

Mount Drasius is cold, very cold, unless you're on the side with the flowing lava. For Derek and Deanna, and their travel partners Tobungus and Zorell, the journey is to the cold side of the mountain. They team up with a band of snowball-throwing kangaroos living near a great temple that just might be the hiding place of the fourth moonstone. Eldrack's magic looks strong enough to finally defeat the twins, until a pair of sweaty socks powers up Deanna's magic.

*The Eye of the Red Dragon: Guardians of Elestra #5* (available July 2011)

The twins and their friends accompany Iszarre to King Barado's castle for a picnic that ends with Iszarre arguing with a peach tree about giving him a second piece of fruit. Their search for the fifth moonstone starts with a trip to Tobungus' home, the Torallian Forest, so Zorell must meditate to find a happy place, and Tobungus needs to feed his shoes flipper juice to increase his dancing abilities. If Tobungus seems weird, his friend Rorrdoogo and the Mushroom wizard Bohootus are stranger yet. But, the real action takes place in the Dragon Realm where a young king finds his way, and his color, and an old dragon gets his mojo back. At the end of their adventure, as usual, Derek and Deanna are left with more questions than answers. Who was this friend who betrayed the older dragon, and where did all of the purple dragon wizards go?

*The Misty Peaks of Dentarus: Guardians of Elestra #6*
(available August 2011)

A trip to the mountains would be a nice way for Derek and Deanna to relax after their first five encounters with Eldrack. Unfortunately, these are the Antikrom Mountains where time occasionally goes in reverse, and where valleys are perfect places for an ambush by Eldrack's forces. The Iron Forest floats above the highest peaks, and the twins learn that sometimes the right jacket is all you need to fly. They meet their uncle the yak farmer who insists that he must stay out of the family's battle against Eldrack. That's too bad because he could tip balance in their favor.

# Author Bio

Thom Jones is the author of the *Guardians of Elestra* series, as well as two forthcoming series, *Galactic Gourmets* (science fiction) and *The Adventures of Boron Jones* (superhero meets chemistry).

He has taught subjects including history, atmospheric science, and criminology at various colleges. What he loves to do most, though, is work with kids, which he does at the crime scene camps he runs. He began writing the *Guardians of Elestra* stories in 2004 for his two sons. The stories evolved, and Tobungus got stranger over the years. He finally decided to start Peekaboo Pepper Books and publish the stories with the view that kids are smart and funny, and that they are more engaged by somewhat challenging vocabulary and mysteries woven throughout the stories they read.

He lives in the Adirondacks with his wife Linda and their three children, Galen, Aidan, and Dinara. He is extremely lucky to have such wonderful editors in Linda, Galen, and Aidan, who have found too many errors to count and have come up with fantastic ideas, even when they don't know it.

51487927R00086

Made in the USA
San Bernardino, CA
23 July 2017